A CROWN SO CURSED

TANYA ANNE CROSBY

OLIVER HEBER BOOKS

Cover Design by Elena Sova

Art by Draženka Kimpel and Creativedust.com

Published by Oliver Heber Books

0 9 8 7 6 5 4 3 2 1

PRAISE FOR THE GOLDENCHILD PROPHECY

"This was the series she was born to write. I am ravenous for the next installment!"

"I've just been inside the mind of a genius. Tanya Anne Crosby is in a class by herself. She creates gorgeous worlds where fact and fiction blend to create a stunning epic. Utterly brilliant."

"A breathtaking true tale with a touch of Celtic magic, brought to life by a soul-stirring storyteller."

"Not simply a romantic fantasy. The characters are complex and do not divulge their thoughts or purpose easily. Crosby has created a balanced, multifaceted genre, one where history's battle cry is tangible while fingers of fable and fantasy pull and tug the unwary."

"Exquisite, lyrical, powerful, and haunting... Gwendolyn of Cornwall's epic journey... will remain in your heart long after you finish the last page."

"Holy Cow! One of my all-time favorite books I have read this year! An absolute masterpiece!"

"A bit of Fae magic, a bit of Arthurian aura... wrapped around a nugget of British history that has almost disappeared into the mist of time."

"An epic story... Tanya breathes life into a timeless tale of love and betrayal, blurring the lines of fantasy and history. "

"Crosby's characters keep readers engaged..."

"Tanya Anne Crosby pens a tale that touches your soul and lives forever in your heart."

SERIES BIBLIOGRAPHY
A BRAND-NEW SERIES

THE GOLDEN PROPHECY

The Cornish Princess

The Queen's Huntsman

The Forgotten Prince

Arise the Queen

A Crown So Cursed

FOREWORD

At this point in my career, I would say that not only is The Goldenchild Prophecy my fave series, it's probably always going to be. This is a story of my heart, and as eager as I am to move on to a new series, I am equally saddened to leave this one behind. However, I left an open thread in this story that could resurface at a later time. See if you can figure out which thread that is.

As for this novella, it isn't necessary to read this to complete the ARC for this series. It exists as a thank you to my romance readers, who followed me into this exciting new genre and who trusted me to entertain, despite that The Goldenchild Prophecy doesn't follow any of the same rules as romance. This slightly naughty extended epilogue is a labor of love for those of you who journeyed with me throughout my years of writing romance.

Additionally, as you read this—especially if you did not read the series—you might become confused by Gwendolyn's identity, as well as her relationships with Malik and

Esme. So here's a quick overview to recap what was revealed in the series: Gwendolyn has three names. One she received upon her birth in the mortal realm, one she was introduced as by her father upon her arrival at the Fae Court, and her true name, known only to a few. She is Gwendolyn of Cornwall, and also Niamh of the Golden Hair, but she is actually Curcog, the daughter of a god. And no, Malik is not Esme's true brother. They were wards of the court together, under Aengus. But Esme and Gwendolyn are blood siblings.

I hope that helps!

And now, please enjoy!

PROLOGUE

Following the death of the mortal tyrant, Locrinus Ap Brwt, the newly crowned Fae king shuttered every remaining portal.

In return for the Shadow Court's aid during the Battle at River Stour, he promised to separate the Fae and mortal kingdoms, parting their destinies evermore.

Assuming a crown he never coveted, the weight of it rested torturously upon his brow, day after day, a reminder of promises made that bound him to this realm. Alas, though it was a long-held belief that the Fae could not lie, this was untrue. He simply could not lie to *her*—and so he remained... beneath a mountain called Regret.

To rule.

To pine.

Lament.

And so, he believed, it should be his penance to yearn for a mortal queen who would forever hold sway over his heart. And meanwhile, in her own realm, Gwendolyn of Cornwall would live and die, and he would live on...and on...and on... with the memory of lost love to haunt him eternally.

After a while, this knowledge turned his heart cold, and through it all, he maintained that icy demeanor because if his heart should ever thaw, he would drown in a floodtide of emotions. His longing consumed him, and he paced the halls of his netherworld palace, a mere shadow of his former self, with the memory of his beloved like a bone-sharp dagger plunged through his undying heart. His penance was his existence—a punishment far worse than any the Shadow Court might adjudge.

No, but, in the wee hours, when *the bean sídhes* wailed, and the wind carried the laments of the lost, he sought solace in the darkest reaches of his mind where his lover's memory dwelt... amidst a sun-scented breeze and swaying daisies.

In a jeweled locket, he kept the proof of their love...

A single golden curl.

Gold and fine.

Soft and light.

Meanwhile, in the mortal realm, the years slip by like too many grains of sand, and the ache in his heart grows more and more profound...even as his voice fades from her memory and hope is all but lost in the labyrinth of his sorrow.

Until...

One day...

Y12,025 A.D. (AFTER DANU)

S ome claim misery loves company.

I assure you; it does not.

It is a nasty little slug that feeds upon the soul, draining it of all hope and life until naught remains but an empty husk.

That's me, surrounded by my feckless court—a kingdom of courtiers who will revel to see me fall. And this will be the night my hope withers and dies.

Every pointy-eared, fang-toothed noble in attendance awaits with bated breath, whispering behind brightly painted lips—all the while whirling and twirling to this gladsome melody that has no bloody hope of ever lifting my disagreeable mood.

The music swells again, and I retrieve the self-replenishing goblet from the table at my side, hoisting it to my lips, then chugging an endless draught.

"*That* won't help," admonishes the Púca.

I answer with a snarl.

As always, the creature speaks true, but that, too, is maddening when I already know that no amount of wine will dull this ache in my heart, regardless of how many times I turn the cup.

But at least it gives my mouth something to do besides yawn.

"I am aware," I mutter beneath my breath, then set down the goblet with a thud. Leaning forward, I rub the bridge of my nose, feeling the onset of a headache that no magic or medicine will cure. "Why are you still here?" I add irascibly.

"Like it or not, I promised to look after you."

My voice itself is a snarl. "Promised whom?"

"Esme," says the Púca, and I mumble an oath.

"Her," I say, the word an epithet by its tenor alone.

We've gone round and round about my long-lost *sister*, and I weary of asking what the creature knows only to have him shift his form every time he means to avoid answering my questions.

If he were not the last of his kind, I would murder him where he lies and be done with his infuriating evasions. "I take it you speak to her?"

He says nothing, only flicks his tail.

"Does she intend to grace us with her presence any day soon?"

In all these years, Esme has not shown her face once.

And neither did she remain in Trevena—I know because I have my spies.

The Fae can no longer traverse the Veil, but there are

ways and means for a king to keep his ears to the ground, supernatural and otherwise. An intricate network of whisperers keeps me informed of events that might sway the already precarious balance of this court.

And yet, of Esme, there is naught but silence—a silence more telling than a thousand spies' reports. Again, the Púca flicks his tail. "I am not your sister's keeper."

"For the last time, *she* is *not* my sister!"

"I am not enjoying your mood."

"So what?"

"Should I take my leave?"

"Please do," I say. Somewhere far from here, I think, but won't say it aloud. Because at the pith of it all, I am alone, and if the Púca should abandon me, I would find myself with one less friend—a commodity I am quickly running out of, in a realm where alliances are as thin as the Veil itself. More to the point, he, she—whatever it is today—is the creature I most trust.

What irony is that?

He's also the most changeable in this land.

Inexplicably, he remains by my side, and I should be grateful for it, but I am too miserable to appreciate aught. Sliding deeper into the Horned Throne, my eyes scrutinize the glittering throng, anticipating betrayal at every turn.

Will I see mutiny if I tarry too long?

Oh, how I despise the machinations!

The ease with which allegiances shift.

And yet, my deepest enmity is reserved for myself.

I am a shadow of the creature I once was—no longer *her*

Shadow, but that is doubtless a role I would resume, only to be at her side. Instead, I am a poor excuse for a king—one who cannot even command loyalty from his subjects, save through fear.

And yes...they *should* fear me, for I have never been more on the verge of becoming my worst self—a monster, in truth, a creature who craves only chaos and ruin...simply to feel.

My hand reaches for the chain about my neck—the one bearing the sliver of Gwendolyn's locks. It would be so easy to give in, to allow the darkness to consume me. But even as the temptation gnaws at my soul, I know I will never succumb—for her sake, not mine.

Gwendolyn always saw the best in me, even when I could not, and my heart is not so dead that I will allow the worst of my kind to assume this throne.

The Fae are lovely, feckless creatures, and there are many among my kind who are not pleased only to see the Fae and mortal worlds divided. They would defy even the gods to destroy humankind. And though I confess there are a few amidst the mortals I would gladly see ended, the Shadow Court's wrath would begin with *her*....

Because *she* dared murder one Fae king...

And steal another's heart.

Mine.

Releasing the chain, I reach for my cup again and seize another bracing mouthful. The goblet refills anew—a parody of plenty for a king who cannot drink enough.

I slam another down hard, splashing crimson on my tunic, and let my gaze prowl the hall...my gaze drawn to one creature in particular, who bears a striking resemblance to her father...save for the hair. Standing beside her dark-haired mother, Lirael Silvershade is a vision to behold, with hair like spun gold, and skin as silky as a dew-kissed rose.

But her tresses lack Gwendolyn's golden fire.

And her eyes are too narrow and guarded.

No matter, she is the bride my Shadow Court would have me take, and every muscle in my body recoils at the notion. This is naught but a politikal exercise to placate the vultures circling my throne. With a snort of disgust, I avert my gaze from the mind-numbing sea of color spinning before my eyes —a magnificent display of intemperance that never fails to bore me.

The sight summons forth a yawn so vast I fear I may swallow the room.

I am jaded, perhaps, and worn, but the weight of this crown has never been so burdensome, nor the weight of my duties ever more suffocating.

The Púca studies me with his cat-*sidhe* eyes reflecting the Faerie Flames—entirely too knowing. Discomfited, I turn away to contemplate the newest tapestry adorning the west wall—a *gift* from my Shadow Court. But unlike the other tapestries gracing this throne-room, that one was not woven by Arachne, nor was it meant to be a fond remembrance of our time in the mortal lands. Rather, it is intended to remind their mortal-loving king of the wonders men were so quick to destroy. One after another, the gallery shifts from one marvel of architecture to another...

A tower lifting unto the heavens.

The pyramids of Al-Ṣaḥrā ' al-Kubrā.

The Hanging Gardens of Bāb-ilim...

In the end, there may be some truth in their complaints. Mortals are destructive in their ignorance and greed, but also capable of creating beauty and wonder.

Gwendolyn is by far the best of them—far better than I— and though the thought does not lessen the burden I carry, it brings a flicker of warmth to my cold heart. Alas, she dwells beyond my reach, in a realm where I cannot follow, severed by more than just distance, and it pains me to consider she may never again walk these halls.

The Púca curses profusely, and the hairs on the back of my neck stand on end.

I turn to meet the High Lord Minister's gaze, and a matching string of oaths rises to my lips. I swallow the words, returning the goblet to its perch, quite certain that my future father-in-law's hearing is as good, if not better, than mine.

Sadly, Lord Elric's familiarity is a testament to his standing in this court; and this is an audacity I must begrudgingly allow.

Stopping before the dais, he casts one glance at the Púca, and though he says nothing about the creature at my side, I sense his condemnation. It spews from his very pores. It matters not that the Púca's breed is rare. To the denizens of this court, his ilk is no more tolerable than a human or a troll. "Majesty," he says.

I lean forward, but otherwise do not respond. Still, I offer my undivided attention.

At my side, the Púca tucks his whiskered face between two paws.

"Do you not find this celebration to your liking?" the High Lord Minister asks, his impatience curling about the corners of his diplomacy. Lord Elric's time in this court harkens back to a time when Nuada of the Silver Arm first sat upon the Horned Throne, and I know Elric, himself, had a hand in his fall... whispering to the Court of his imperfections, turning our kindred against him, Seelie and Unseelie alike. There is only one thing that keeps him from withdrawing his support... and that is the possibility of his daughter's ascension to the vacant seat at my side.

"Define enjoyment," I retort, and the elder smiles thinly.

Between us, an insult lies, and I wonder if it will rise to his tongue.

"For some," he expounds, his tone patronizing, though veiled enough to befit the decorum of our exchange. "It seems the concept of enjoyment remains but a fleeting notion, forever out of reach, as one yearns for things that cannot be?"

And there it is.

Fomorian blackguard.

My fists clench at the barb beneath his words. We both know of whom and what he speaks. "I have no patience for riddles, Lord Elric."

"Of course not," he allows. "But as you must know, Majesty, the court grows weary..."

I peer at the dancers to find no evidence of that, but his lips twist into another form of a smile, this one more akin to a smirk, and he says, "As does my daughter."

"She is not the only contender," I remind him, my voice as cold as the chill of my empty bed.

The High Lord Minister's cheeks stain crimson. With his lips pursed, he peers down at his shoes, sliding his long-clawed fingers behind his back. "Yes, well... forgive me, Majesty."

And then, his smile sharpens, a blade honed on centuries of courtly intrigue. "She is not. But the question remains, Lord King, how long will you allow this indecision to fester?"

Again, I lean forward. But words do not come. Instead, I allow the silence to swell between us, laden as it is with the weight of unspoken threats and the fragile construction of alliances that may shatter with one wrong word.

Lord Elric bows—a gesture so minutely executed it borders on insolence. "I am certain I needn't remind you. It is only my influence that keeps you on the throne."

My silence stretches, heavy and unyielding. I can feel the Púca's gaze upon me, its weight almost tangible, but the creature remains silent, an observer in this game of thorns.

"Left to their own devices," he continues. "There are many who would vote no confidence... and yet...if you might only see your way to choose... A queen will provide a measure of stability for this court. She will give us a reason to unite and perhaps lay to rest the specter of dissension that has too long haunted these halls." The undercurrent in his voice implies more than a simple plea for unity; it carries a veiled threat. I stare at him, feeling the frost in my veins threaten to crack.

There is nothing I can say that will improve the situation.

I lean back now, imagining our parlay as a game of Queen's Chess.

A game I am losing.

Or rather, a game I have already lost.

I am only reluctant to move my last piece.

But stalling will only serve me for so long.

"Fret not," I concede. "I will choose, but not at the expense of the throne's dignity, or my own. What would you have me do? Pluck a bride from this crowd as I would a piece of ripened fruit?"

He smiles. "If you wait too long, fruit may rot, and there may be consequences for that."

Again, I lean forward, daring him to speak more plainly. "What consequence?"

Lord Elric's obsidian eyes narrow, a hint of the tactical mind he is renowned for flashing briefly as he considers my retort. "The continuation of your lineage, of course, the stability of our realm—both for the better if you do as the Court requests?"

More like... demands.

There is no choice to be made here, and I know it.

He pauses for effect. "Unless there are other...*factors* at play?"

I sigh, then sit back, disappointed that the jeweled blade at my boot will not find a good use this eve. "I am aware of my duties, Lord Elric. You needn't remind me."

"I wouldn't presume," he replies. "It is simply that...I believed we had an understanding?"

"I will choose when I am ready," I say again. "Not a

moment before. For now, I am *enjoying* the..." I search for a word to describe the night's decadence. "Celebration."

The High Lord Minister's eyes glint, though he quickly masks his annoyance with a veneer of subservience. "Yes, of course, Majesty. I meant no offense."

"You will have your way," I reassure him, and he nods, and satisfied with that, turns on his heels, his pointy ears twitching.

Indeed, those overly long ears are a testament to his age —the points extending well above his golden sheaths. It is a lesser-known fact...Elvin ears elongate as we age, and I know the High Lord Minister resents the small points of mine—a stripling youth who never coveted the crown or the throne, and who cannot even be bothered to choose a mate for the sake of the realm.

But they clamor for a queen, and I have promised to give them one.

"He is right, you know," says the Púca, piping up now that Lord Elric has gone. "If you allow it, this *celebration* will continue in perpetuity," he advises. "Those dancers will spin for eternity. And regardless, for the sake of this court, you must eventually choose."

I wave a hand dismissively. "One thing you can be sure of...when the subject of heirs has arisen betwixt immortals, it is only because they are already plotting my death."

"You cannot know this for certain."

"Oh, I do!" I laugh without humor. "Lest you forget, during Aengus' final days, all the same voices were crooning the same song. And now, it is my turn."

"It could be they simply want a bride to soften your temper?"

I say nothing, and he continues.

"There is little reassuring about your demeanor of late. You've sat on that throne for too long without a mate. If it is Gwendolyn you covet, remedy this. Or resign yourself to doing as they ask."

Every word of my reply sits on a knife's edge. "I said I would not return to *that place*." My voice is a rumble of thunder. "I will not, even for her."

"You would if she had but asked?"

"But she did not," I say, and the Púca sighs, his whiskers twitching loudly.

"Well, then...you have an answer."

I toss him a glare. "I did not ask you a question."

"You may not avoid the Fates, Málik. Give the wretches the queen they long for, and be done. You know I speak true. The longer you delay, the more precarious your position."

In this realm, there are many ways to kill a king even without resorting to slitting his throat as he sleeps...again, I know he speaks true. My wards are only as good as the guards I have employed, and their loyalties are sure to be tested.

The Púca's words hang between us.

"The Shadow Court will see you dead if you defy them any longer. If not for your sake, for the sake of this realm, choose a bride and be done," he argues.

I turn my gaze from Elric, meeting his daughter's violet eyes. She waves excitedly, encouraging me to join the revelry, and I offer a nod devoid of sincerity.

Gods know, now is as good a time as any.

For all her father's posturing, without a proper heir, it is he himself who would displace me.

And so we begin...

She is not here.

She is not coming.

And there is nothing anyone can do about it.

Not even me...

CHAPTER
TWO

J ust as predicted, a portal appeared along the horizon, its rim all but lost in the blush of sunlight, so that for a moment, it seemed nothing more than a trick of the clouds—a mere shimmer, pale and fleeting.

Crossing her arms against the cool, brisk wind, Gwendolyn inhaled a salt-laden breath, anticipation tickling at her belly like a thousand *piskie* wings.

How desperately she longed to see him!

To reach out.

Touch him.

Trace the sharp contours of his face...

Throughout these twenty-two years, she had met no one who could make her feel the way he did. No one who could set her blood afire. No one consumed her thoughts as completely as did Málik from the moment their eyes met across the courtyard in Trevena.

Remembering, she closed her eyes...

He was so damned arrogant—so full of himself, so insufferably haughty, and perhaps it was all the worse because Gwendolyn had loved him from the very first, despite that he'd barely spared her a glance.

To her, he was no less than a god—every hair atop his head utterly divine.

But to him? She had been—at least so she'd believed—a burdensome task, foisted upon him by her father. The humiliation of it still burned in her chest. How furious she had been when her father demoted Bryn and assigned Málik in his stead. She'd sworn to show Málik no mercy, and yet, repeatedly, he'd bested her on the court, putting her flat on her back and leaving her a sweaty, unhappy mess—not that her misery could be blamed solely on the sparring. Even now, her pulse quickened as she recalled the way his lithe body moved, so graceful and sure, his bastard sword flickering like quicksilver beneath the afternoon sun. Even when she'd tried to convince herself she despised him—loathed him—she had been utterly captivated by the power and beauty of his form...

And all the while, she burned to defeat him.

To prove herself worthy of his notice.

To force him—if only for a moment—to see her.

It wasn't until much later that she'd learned the truth of his feelings, and even now, she remembered the shock in his *icebourne* eyes as he watched the snips of her hair tumble like golden leaves into her lap... eyes wide with mortification over what it revealed...

True love—the kind that transcends all.

And yet so much had happened since that day, and Gwendolyn feared the time they had spent apart. But she dared to hope...

Did he long for her as she did for him?

That day—so long ago now, it seemed another life—on the blood-soaked fields outside Lundinium, she had so much wished for him to turn, just once. To look back. And if he had —if he'd so much as glanced over his shoulder—she would have gone after him. Gods, she would have run. Crown be damned. Aisling be damned. But he never did. He rode away, and with him, took a piece of Gwendolyn's heart. The memory of his back, his broad shoulders shrinking into the mist, haunted her even now—like a wound that never healed.

Perhaps in some secret place, she had longed to rip off her father's crown and chase after him, to let the world burn for all she cared.

But queens did not chase lovers.

Not even be they kings.

So she had stood there, watching him go.

Alas...twenty-two years was a long time, and her face was no longer given to the bloom of youth. Her golden curls were not so bright and bore a few strands of gray. Her face was beginning to reveal lines at the corners of her eyes and mouth, and for all that she had lived, the wide-eyed wonder of her youth had long-since faded, replaced by a more thoughtful gaze.

Would he still find her lovely, as he'd once claimed?

Gwendolyn was not so vain, but she knew age would not have touched his face, and she wished so much that she could turn back time. Closing her eyes, she allowed the salt mist to spray her face as she whispered a fervent prayer to every god who would listen.

Please, please...do not let him forget me.

Gwendolyn no longer knew what she believed. So much of what she had learned though experience, gave lie to the Awenydds' tales. And no matter that she herself had spent some time in the Underlands, the years now left her uncertain. Were it not for the cloak she wore and the Sword of Light she gave to Habren, she would have had nothing to prove her time in the Underlands was not simply a fevered dream.

Absently, her fingers stroked the threads of the Orb Weaver's cloak, remembering the day Arachne had given it to her. The spider woman's obsidian eyes had glittered with knowing as she'd pressed the coat into Gwendolyn's hands —a cloak meant to shield her true form from the Fae king's sight, and now she wondered...

Would it soften her age?

Would it allow him to see her as she once was? Or perhaps, would it reveal the truth of the years that had passed, the lines etched by worry and longing more than any physical aging?

The portal before her shimmered more vibrantly now, its edges blurring with the colors of dawn. A storm was brewing, and Manannán had already warned her that if they did not reach the portal in time, it would be another turning of the season before it would open again, but not to the place she most wished to go.

Four times every year, those portals appeared, each time

to a different realm—once to the Isle of Mona, another to the Underlands, another to Hyperborea, and the ultimate time to the Lands of Eternal Winter. But though Manannán could command the portals, he could never pass through them himself. That was his curse. They were his to command, but never to traverse.

So he claimed, and so it was—every god held that power, or so they believed. Yet whether they themselves were welcome on the far side of the Veil was not for them to decide. That, he said, depended upon the hearts of those who dwelt within. The judgment belonged to them alone.

The sound of Manannán's voice startled her from her reverie.

"We haven't much time," he said, approaching. "Art ready?"

"I am," Gwendolyn replied, spinning to face him.

Theirs was a fledgling relationship, born of her desire to see Málik, but, to Gwendolyn's surprise, Manannán was not what she had once supposed. A sea god he might be, but here and now, standing alongside her, she found his heart in his eyes.

He was simply an old man—one she'd been parted from for too long.

"You must beware," he said, worry clouding his tone. "The path you've set upon is not without perils. And, as I've said, Gwendolyn, I can only carry you to the threshold. Once you disembark, I will have no means to defend you, nor even to retrieve you... not without help."

"I understand," she said, resolved, and the old man sighed.

His voice was gruff with disguised emotion. "Remember your lessons! The Fae are overly capricious, with *politiks* more twisted than a wych elm!"

She did not doubt his warning, but she laughed at the finger he wagged. "There is no danger I would not face... for him," she reassured.

During her time Below, Gwendolyn had encountered more than a few foes. But none so chilling as the denizens of the Fae Court themselves, whose unsparing gazes she would not soon forget.

At no point had she felt welcome in that vipers' nest, and she bore no illusions they would be pleased with her return. No doubt. Were they to have it their way, she would find herself in another gilded cage. And no matter—her gaze returned to the shimmering portal—she would brave anything for the promise of Málik's arms.

Manannán's voice, when he spoke, was heavy with regret. "There is also this to consider... after all the years we've spent apart, your decision also means you and I may never meet again."

At this, a pang of sorrow pierced Gwendolyn, sharp and sudden.

During the short time they'd spent together, she cherished his wisdom and gentle guidance.

For all the brevity of their acquaintance, she treasured his wisdom, the gentle cadence of his guidance, and the comfort of his presence. The months spent waiting for the portal's return had passed in long, meandering conversations— about the Fae rebellion, about his place among the gods, about his exile from the Underlands. He told her everything, it seemed, except anything about herself, and always with the same excuse: that he was forbidden to speak of her life before Trevena.

It surprised her, then, to learn that the one to whom he was sworn was Gwendolyn herself. She could not forgive the oath she'd forced upon him, unwittingly or not, as his daughter. Worse still, she had bound him never to seek her, and the duty he bore was not merely loyalty, but a transaction—one that bound him beyond even a god's decree. Whatever it was he kept from her, he believed it would endanger her in the Underlands. And so, she was left with only questions, and the ache of knowing that, by her own hand, she might have lost him forever.

"Does Málik know about this thing you will not speak of?" she'd asked him.

Silence was his response, and again when she'd inquired about Esme. His silence had been heavy, almost pregnant with unspoken words.

"There are things beyond even my reach, Child," he'd said at last, his voice subdued, edged with regret. Manannán was nothing like her mortal father, but Gwendolyn cared for him just the same, and the thought of never seeing him again genuinely aggrieved her.

She met his gaze now, her blue eyes awash with tears, and reached out to clasp his hands in her own. "Words can never express my gratitude for everything you have done...for all you will do. But I *need* to go." In fact, standing on the precipice of her old life and the possibilities of a new one, Gwendolyn felt a strange mix of fear and exhilaration. No doubt, it would be a dangerous quest, navigating the intrigues of the Fae Court—a den of creatures impetuous enough to destroy her on a whim, but she was resolute. "Promise me you'll take care," she implored, her voice thick with emotion.

Manannán nodded, his voice failing him. He released her hand, reaching up to brush at her cloak. "Then you must take care," he said finally, tears hazing his eyes.

Her greatest test, he then assured, would lie within the Unseelie Court, whose members stood for traditions that were against Gwendolyn's very existence. They would not turn a blind eye to a human and Fae union, and no matter what Gwendolyn was in her past life, she was still a mortal.

"Dark and manipulative, with loyalties woven from grievances more than love and honor, the Shadow Court will oppose you from the moment you arrive," he said. "They will watch you with daggers drawn, prepared to strike at any sign of weakness."

"Then I will not be weak," she swore.

They would not find her a simpering miss—not when, as a youth, and a woman, Gwendolyn had defeated all of Pretania's rebels, along with the Usurper she'd married, to shape a nation. And any danger she would face Below would be inconsequential in the face of her greatest desire of all—to see Málik again, to hold him, to tell him she loved him still.

Three times he had begged her to go away with him, and three times she had denied him. His face after refusing him the last time would haunt Gwendolyn till the day she died—mayhap sooner than later if she placed herself at odds with the Shadow Court.

And still Manannán persisted, a note of melancholy in

his voice. "The daughter of a god may have any man in all four kingdoms. Art certain, Gwendolyn?"

Her answer was swift. "More than ever."

A long moment of silence unfurled between them.

Manannán mac Lir attempted to speak, but words again failed him, and a sting of tears needled at Gwendolyn's eyes —no less sharp for the knowledge that she, too, would soon abandon everything and everyone she had ever known. All her friends, all her allies... even her son, and Cornwall, too. The thought of it hollowed her, but she held her tongue.

Her father regarded her with a sober, searching gaze— his ancient eyes reflecting the gray tumult of the sea itself. He said nothing, but Gwendolyn understood well enough what she was asking of him: to relinquish any hope of mending the bond with his estranged daughter. It was no small thing. She managed a wistful smile, her lips trembling.

"May I convey your greetings to the Púca?"

His old eyes crinkled at the corners. "Please do. Tell that curious little beast hello when you see him—and you will, sooner than me!"

It was a complaint, to be sure, though he did not voice it as such. Instead, he flashed a bright, wolfish smile. "Come along then!"

Gwendolyn's heart leapt—then stuck, quivering, in her throat as he seized her hand and drew her after him, down the narrow path to the lonely spit of beach, where he kept his precious boat: *Sguaba Tuinne*—The Wave Sweeper. Infamous it was, though in truth, only an old coracle—a mean little barque, all wickerwork and blackened bitumen, as though any amount of pitch could keep such a vessel from leaking.

To even think of braving the sea in that wicked little bowl was madness. Yet she had come with him from Cornwall to the Isle of Man in it, and knew better than most what the coracle could endure. It was stronger than it looked. Its oars were mere ornament—tokens for the uninitiated. The boat was enchanted, attuned to its master's thoughts, and would turn or speed or slow at the merest whim. The ocean itself bent to Manannán's whispers, and the little boat obeyed.

As Gwendolyn stepped into the boat, the vessel rocked gently beneath her feet, and she quickly settled herself onto a wooden bench in the back, her fingers curling about the boat's edges as Manannán pushed the skiff into the surf. Waves lapped at the gunwales, and when they were far enough out, Manannán jumped in and took his seat, his gnarled, old hands grasping the oars that would help navigate them safely across the Minch and through the Veil between worlds.

"One last time for us," he said with a wry smile, and together in silence, they traversed the roiling deep, the sky a somber blanket of smoke, and the air crisp with the scent of the sea.

Manannán applied the oars in sync with the ocean, every stroke a verse in a poem only he understood. As they rowed out across the waves, with the wind whipping through her hair, Gwendolyn's heart pounded with anticipation and a bit of fear.

Above, the sky became a churning mass of blustering clouds, but beneath the brewing chaos, Manannán whistled as he rowed, his every stroke sending the small skiff rolling over the waves like a feather in a tempest. Their destination lay at the heart of the sea, and as they approached the portal, the winds grew. Gwendolyn glanced back one last time at the receding shoreline, feeling for the first time the true magnitude of her decision.

If she dared cross through, she would never again set eyes on her sweet son...

Nor Bryn.

Nor Taryn.

Nor Ely.

The weight of this truth pulled at her heart, but the image of Málik brought with it a new flood of longing as the air crackled with magic.

Thunder.

Lighting.

The sound raised the little hairs on Gwendolyn's arms.

"Hold!" Manannán cried over the roar. "Hold!"

Like a rag doll, the tiny skiff was tossed by the fury of the ocean. Still, her father's arms remained steady as he shouldered against their force. "We are merely tested," he said with a grin, and Gwendolyn seized the edges of the boat as the world itself rocked, then spun.

She really wasn't sure.

At long last, the moment of truth—when the magic of her father's enchanted vessel would test the boundaries of the Fae and mortal realms...even against his raging sea.

Every push, every mighty swell was like a battle cry between warring worlds, guarding against trespassers. But for all their fury, nothing could hold back Manannán mac Lir, whose feat of strength was unmatched amidst gods, old and new.

The world burst into a prism of color as they plunged through the portal, and Gwendolyn clung to *Sguaba Tuinne*, her knuckles turning white. She felt a familiar surge, a pulse so formidable it tugged at her soul...and then...

Silence.

CHAPTER
THREE

Bedecked for the occasion, every aspect of the King's Hall has been artfully designed to mirror a world my kind has been denied.

Portieres billow with an unseen breeze, fronds of green spill over the edges of urns, their twisting roots escaping across the floor, as though the woodlands sought to reclaim this space from which it had been so long banished.

Most maddening of all is that wretched ceiling—a living masterpiece accurately depicting the cycles of day and night, complete with sunrises and sunsets painted in every shade of its creation. Some hours ago, I commanded that cycle's disruption, declaring that, for the remainder of these "festivities," it should remain a never-ending length of night...

Dark and joyless.

Like my mood.

And if anyone should wonder how long the Fae can dance... my last count before commanding those cycles to end numbered eight-thousand, thirty...

One.

For.

Every.

Mortal.

Day.

I.

Have.

Borne.

Without.

Her.

More than twenty-two years have passed since I last glimpsed Gwendolyn's face, and still the pain of our parting hasn't dulled one gob. It has simply transformed, reshaping itself into this cancerous sorrow that spreads through my veins with every beat of my immortal heart.

How old is she now?

Forty-one? Two?

Her life will pass in the blink of an eye, and regardless, I will love her at seventy, her blue eyes dulled by age, and even into the grave, when there is naught left but bones.

And make no mistake, I *would* crawl into that tomb, and there remain if I could.

Do you think I would not?

If so, then you have forgotten I am a monster—a sordid creature only saved by the heart that now beats only for her. No empyreal decree nor courtly machination can steer the course of a love so deep, so all-consuming, it does not recognize the passing of decades, but grows stronger with each passing day.

If I could command it so, I would halt time's relentless

march, keeping her vibrant and fierce, with laughter that could light the darkest corners of any realm.

But I cannot.

And I have already put off this decision for too long.

Lirael's eyes brighten as I shove my arse out of the throne.

Joy?

Triumph?

I curse silently, imagining the machinations to come.

She is her father's daughter, after all, and whilst she might have presented a facade of gentility to this court, I know that gleam in her eyes—a blinding, diamond-hard ambition that outshines any jewel in this hall. But this is a malady that consumes us all. We are Fae, and greed is the marrow of our bones, the root of our banishment, the silent architect of every wound we have ever caused or suffered. We are not creatures of harmony; we are the children of acquisitiveness, grown monstrous in our exile, forever denied the world we crave.

I see myself in Lirael's ambition, and in that cruel reflection I recognize every ancestor who ever lived, every offspring who will ever be born. Without Gwendolyn, I am simply another link in the same unbreakable chain.

My legs grow heavy with the gravity of my decision, and the court's attention shifts. Every eye now turns to me. Every face—painted in the cold light of a false moon—betrays a singular, primal anticipation. With leaden steps, I move to the edge of the dais, then pause, my gaze drifting across the assembled. And for all anyone knows, I have paused merely to allow the import of this moment to settle, but it is to still my beating heart.

I will speak the words, then die a little, even as Lirael smiles.

My hands clench and unclench at my sides as I dare to meet Lord Elric's gaze.

Gods know. If there were any hope for joy—any at all apart from my beloved—I would choose a bride other than Lord Elric's simpering daughter. But even as I consider this, I know I will not. If I cannot have Gwendolyn, a union with Lirael will serve its purpose, even if thereafter, I will become a puppet king. I will command the military, and matters of High Law, but what I eat, how I eat it, where I eat it, and with whom shall be dictated by *her*. *She* will be the master of my demesne, and I, her unwilling slave—a huntsman again, only this time for an unworthy queen.

Choking down my bitterness, I begin. "Ladies...lords of this court..." My smile is tight, insincere. "As you all know...this occasion is long overdue..."

My regard turns to Lirael, standing tall in her costume of silks, so confident in her victory. Unflinching, her eyes meet mine as the rest of the court draws a breath.

My answering smile is forced, and the words taste like ash in my mouth, "The realm has too long been without an heir," I add, flicking a glance toward Lord Elric and the odious smirk that carves its way across his visage is as intolerable to me as his *politiks*. I yearn to wipe it off his face. A few bawdy jokes filter to my ears, but I've no impetus to laugh. There is no humor here, and nothing appealing about the thought of bedding Lirael Silvershade.

Nothing about her stirs my passion

I do not thrill over the thought of progeny borne of her womb.

The weight of the moment is lost to no one.

"I have...at last...chosen...*your* queen."

Theirs, not mine. I pause, drawing a breath to steel myself for the words to come...words that will forever seal my fate. Indeed, if for us words are binding, vows are indissoluble. Once betrothed, our destinies will be inextricably bound, and the only thing that may free me is death—hers or mine. The only reason I am free to choose again is that, by making herself a changeling, Gwendolyn broke our bond. It matters not that I've shared with her my essence. As a mortal, she will never be my soulmate, no matter how much I wish it.

Anticipation churns through the air like a storm on the verge of breaking.

The court waits in silence, eager to devour my words.

Even the Faerie Flames freeze in their dance.

"I choose—"

The doors to the hall burst wide with a resounding smash, and a collective gasp reverberates through the gathered.

My head whips about.

I feel *her* before I see her.

Gwendolyn.

Standing in the entrance of my hall, her presence commands the attention of every creature within, including mine—most decidedly mine.

Blink, I command myself.

Can it be?

Gods. Nay...

The jolt of seeing her again after so long strikes me like a bolt of lightning, leaving me momentarily mute, and my mind a tempest of emotions.

Lovely as ever, she stands poised at the threshold, her fiery tresses cascading about her shoulders like a torrent of fire. Her gray eyes sparkle with a touch of defiance, and her gaze finds me, provoking a surge of emotions so powerful I stagger slightly where I stand.

But in the space of that eternal moment, as our eyes meet, my heart pounds, and my blood sings. She smiles, and the sight of it robs me of my breath.

Dressed plainly compared to the denizens of my court, the lack of ornamentation only serves to enhance her natural beauty. Her eyes, stormy as ever, but driven, scan the gathered nobility, holding everyone—including me—enthralled.

"Pardon," she says.

No one replies.

Not even me.

At long last, she has come, and I am as inept as a babe, unable to speak, even to reassure her, or even to greet her.

"I...seek...an audience...with...your king," she says haltingly, speaking at large to my court, while her gaze is fixed on mine. All eyes turn to me, awaiting my response—to oust her from this hall, no doubt. But there is one thing I know as surely as I breathe...*I will not.*

"Approach," I say, then wince, because I am a mindless cretin—undone by the mere sight of her. My voice, when it escapes, is harsher than it needs to be to cover my awkwardness.

She lifts her chin, at once complying, crossing the hall, parting my courtiers like the queen she is, and I can't help but grin—the first genuine expression of joy in all the years since we parted.

The court hums, the sound rising like a tide of discontent. I pay them no heed, all my attention focused on this woman who'd once dared stand up, not only to me and that foolish mortal she'd once wed, but to Aengus as well.

Indeed, the last time she stood in this very hall, Aengus' head found itself at my feet...and now she advances with the same fearless resolve. Every step echoes across the polished stone floor, resonating within my body, and returning a measure of life to my once-dead heart.

Thump.

Thump.

Thump.

It hurts to breathe, but the ache feels like a sweet torture as it renews sensations long forgotten. Her proximity, the very air that swirls around her, is intoxicating, and with every step she takes toward me, the world seems to right itself after long being askew. My courtiers whisper among themselves, their voices a cacophony of indignation...

"It cannot be!"

"That's her!"

"Banríon na bhfear!"

"Why is *she* here?"

And so on, and so on...

A tide of protests rises as they recognize her—older now, with a measure of wisdom etched into those once-youthful features. There is newfound maturity in her carriage. But her fire remains.

"Kingslayer!" someone shouts, and my guards advance.

I lift a hand, commanding them to a halt.

At once, they obey, placing hands upon the hilts of their swords, ready to draw at my command.

Again, I will not.

If Gwendolyn came to me now with sword in hand, commanding me to kneel, I would lay myself prostrate at her feet.

Lirael stiffens as she passes, a mask of fury settling over her delicate features, her too-blue eyes narrowing to slits as she watches Gwendolyn with barely concealed malice.

Lord Elric stiffens, too, his smug expression dissolving into one of surprise, then contempt, and he leans into his daughter to administer words of prudence.

It is still my court; one word from me would see them arrested. For all his power and influence, he does not yet possess my crown.

Gwendolyn never hesitates in her stride, and I'd have flown down those bloody stairs to sweep her into my arms, but I suddenly fear I've lost my mind.

What else might explain her presence here when the portals are idle?

Surely this is a dream? But if it is, I should never wake...

And then I scent her...the evidence of our bond—as real and true as the blood that courses through my veins.

I once warned her that our mating would mark her as mine, and there it is, like the lingering refrain of a half-remembered melody I cannot will away, no matter how I try.

The shape and substance of it floods my senses, sweet as blood oranges at high summer.

It is not a mere human memory, nor the feeble chemistry of mortals.

It is a living thing, the ancient magic of our kindred, a thread woven deeper than conscious thought. And though I know the bond should have faded after all these years—should have withered like so much neglected vine, it thrums with life and I am overwhelmed by it, nearly brought to my knees by its relentless certainty.

The crown, my Shadow Court, the bitter eyes of every peer and pretender—none of it matters beside this echoing pulse. I cannot remember if I ever felt so alive...or so vulnerable.

The court, for all its pride, senses it too.

Some shrink back as though burned.

Others lean in with a kind of hungry awe.

Her eyes hold mine—a myriad of emotions swirling within their depths.

Two thoughts assault my brain at once—one of relief, and one of dread...for chaos is what she brings today, even if she comes in peace.

For a moment, the entire world holds its breath.

The whispers of my court fade away.

All I see is her—the one who haunts my dreams.

And the sight of her fills me with a wild, reckless hope.

CHAPTER
FOUR

Resplendent in black, dressed in attire that hinted at the import of this occasion, Málik stood atop the King's Dais, the Horned Crown perched upon his brow. And seeing him there, Gwendolyn was seized by a terrible sense of déjà vu with the courtiers crowding the hall, attired in the most lavish of finery, their silks and jewels glittering beneath the torchlight.

She could not look away from Málik.

There was a question in his eyes—his blink one of surprise. But then, just as swiftly, the shock in his gaze hardened into something altogether inscrutable, and her belly plunged.

It was as though the air itself thickened; the moment stretching taut between them, and Gwendolyn could not help but wonder what he saw when he looked at her now, clothed in her mother's wedding gown and the battered cloak given to her by Arachne.

She braced herself, heart pounding, as she waited for whatever would come next.

Was he displeased at seeing her after so long?

Had she misjudged their bond?

Let her heart lead her into folly?

Gwendolyn stood unsure of herself.

Uncertain what to say next.

Uncertain what to do.

Between them stood his courtiers, caught mid-motion like terrible, beautiful statues, their faces a study in shock. But the moment they registered who had dared interrupt their revels, the change was swift and ugly: lips peeled back to show porbeagle teeth, anger drawing their mouths tight, eyes narrowing with naked loathing. For a heartbeat, the air thickened with their hatred, and not one of them bothered to hide it—not from him, nor from each other.

Clearly, she had interrupted some grand affair. The hush that fell was suffocating, but—she swallowed—she was here now, and she would not be moved until she had said what she came to say.

No matter how many eyes turned to her, no matter how the courtiers bristled at her intrusion, Gwendolyn set her jaw and stood her ground. The air was thick with expectation, and for a moment, she almost faltered, but she forced herself to breathe. It was not as though she could vanish, nor would she wish to. Let them glare. Let them whisper behind their jeweled hands. She would not be cowed by their disdain. Her heart thudded in her chest, but she would endure their scrutiny, their little barbs and jests, until her purpose was fulfilled. If she must stand, alone, before the assembled court, then so be it. She would not yield—not now, not ever. She lifted her chin, refusing to betray her nerves. Here, she would stay, and she would speak, even if it cost Gwendolyn her life.

Only then, when her message was delivered, would she allow herself to go.

Not before.

Already, she'd given up too much.

It was too late to turn back.

Her father made it known that he could not return before the turning of the season; and therefore, if Málik turned her away, Gwendolyn would have nowhere to go.

Gods. The thought of wandering those dark, endless passages gave her a chill, but she did not allow anyone to see her fear. Lifting her chin, she met Málik's gaze, her fingers curling into fists as she took another steadying breath, her heart hammering painfully.

Gods knew she needed to say something—explain her presence—but her voice was lost.

And really, she hadn't intended to speak her heart in front of so many witnesses...

Or with so many glares fixed upon her.

Twenty-two years...

He was not the same—and yet...he was. The years had hardened him. She could tell by the steel in his jaw. He was breathtakingly beautiful, and she begged him with her eyes to know why she'd come.

She loved him—purely, desperately, and without reservation.

Another blink, and his expression softened, the icy gaze thawing a fraction.

What was she doing?

Gwendolyn could not have said, Only that when Málik's lips parted—when words failed him and he stood, silent and stricken—a voice somewhere deep within her commanded her to go to him.

Before she could think, her feet were moving, boots striking the stone floor with a sharp, ringing echo. Courtiers parted for her, a glittering sea of silks and jewels, their indignant whispers prickling at her back. She ignored them all, her eyes fixed on Málik, and when the guards—alerted by her approach—reached for the hilts of their swords, she did not slow, nor did she falter.

Let them try to stop her.

As a matter of habit, her own hand sought the cold steel of her blade; but having arrived unarmed, it slid helplessly to her side and she kept moving, even as her mind spun remembrances of the last time she'd presented herself before this court—another day, before another Fae king. That day, as today, the hall had been filled with lords and ladies with painted faces and glittering attire. Málik had stood upon that very dais, near to where he stood right now, and the ache of his betrayal—the mind-numbing fear over what she thought he might do—now conspired to make pudding of her knees. Gods knew the love in his eyes had been so apparent then. And despite that, duty-bound to his court, he would have taken her head.

"*Would you have done it?*" she'd once asked him.

"*Yes,*" he'd whispered.

And Gwendolyn knew it was true; he would have sliced her head from her shoulders, even if the act would shatter his soul, and knowing that, she felt her heart break anew the closer she drew, finding it suddenly difficult to breathe. Her dread became a living thing, coiling itself about her throat like a serpent, constricting her breath. This time, there was no prospect of retrieving any sword.

This time, she stood alone.

The Fae hissed violently among themselves, their gazes darting betwixt their king and the mortal who'd once more dared to show herself before *their* court.

And this time, Gwendolyn was completely defenseless—without even a proper defense for her heart. But should Málik forsake her, he might as well take her head, for without him, the future was as gray as the winter skies over Fowey Moor.

A tall, willowy Fae suddenly stepped in front of Gwendolyn, impeding her progress—an older creature with eyes like shards of diamonds. "How are you here?" she asked, her words sharp as the dagger in her pretty jeweled belt.

Beside her stood an elder male, and a young female with eyes so bright a blue they were luminescent against her pale skin.

All three of their gazes were trained upon Gwendolyn, their expressions a unified mask of disdain. But Gwendolyn wanted no trouble.

Still, she knew it would not suit her to back down, and neither would she implicate Manannán—not that the Fae could do aught to a god, but if she poisoned them against her father, she might truly never see him again.

"My explanations are the king's alone to hear," she said, emboldened, because, no matter how he felt about her, Málik would never allow her to be persecuted without giving her a chance to defend herself. To be sure, she cast a glance at the dais to find him watching her curiously.

"Now," she said, turning to the courtier again. "Let me pass."

When that failed to impress, Gwendolyn drew herself up to her full height and said, "Or would you like to hand me a blade?" Gods knew she had no desire to provoke the Fae, but she understood instinctively that they would never respect a mortal who cowered. She wanted it clear: she had come unarmed, but she would not yield.

The lady's eyes narrowed.

Well... *lady* was the fairest description.

The creature standing before her was hardly human, and "woman" did not quite suit her. Black of hair, her eyes were also dark and piercing. She laid her hand upon the hilt of her dagger, and smiled, and the tension in the air thickened, palpable as a Cornish mist.

Another heartbeat of silence passed.

And then another.

And finally—as though a levee burst—the lady stepped back, and the hall erupted into babel.

One glance at the dais revealed Málik's half-smile, and then, at last, his voice cut through the caterwauling like a scythe through silk. "Silence!"

The whispers quieted at once.

All eyes turned to the king, awaiting his decree.

So did Gwendolyn's, her nerves frayed.

"Come," he said, crooking a finger at her, and without another word to the courtier, Gwendolyn bolted past her, hurrying toward the dais.

"Mother! Father! Stop her!"

At Gwendolyn's back, the cacophony swelled, a tempest of shock and indignation; and still she hurried toward Málik, her eyes never leaving his.

"Come," he said again once she'd ascended the stairs, and he waited patiently until she joined him, then another moment to be sure no one would follow. And without another word, he pushed Gwendolyn through a billowing partition, away from prying eyes.

The moment they were alone, he turned to face her, drawing Gwendolyn into his arms, holding her close, his body trembling even as did hers—so achingly familiar.

"Málik," she breathed.

"You've come!"

Overwhelmed by emotion, Gwendolyn could only nod, words failing her entirely. How long she had prayed for this moment—how fervently she had longed to be in his arms.

And here she was.

"How? The portals—"

"I know," she said.

"The last time—"

"I know," Gwendolyn interrupted again, guessing at what he would say before he could say it, and her heart swelled with a bittersweet ache, remembering every occasion he'd begged her to go away with him...the first time on the promontory on the return from Chysauster, then again on the ramparts in Trevena, and one last time on the fields before Lundinium.

To every occasion, she had replied: "*No.*"

"*Mo ghrá,*" he whispered—*my love.*

And the sound of those two beauteous words filled Gwendolyn's eyes with tears.

Unable to resist, she clung to him, inhaling his scent—that all-too familiar blend of male spice that was uniquely his. It filled her senses, spurred memories of stolen moments and whispered promises—promises broken only by circumstance, but never forgotten.

"Without you, the years have been an endless winter," he said hoarsely.

"I..." She drew back, searching his face. "I was afraid—"

"Never," he swore, and his eyes glinted with tears.

Even after all these years, the bond was strong enough for them to know each other's sentiments, and his voice softened as he reasoned with her.

"Have I not said, Gwendolyn...you've been my weakness for a hundred thousand years? What are twenty-two measly years against the eternity of my love for you?"

His hands framed her face, the touch feather-light, his fingers tracing the lines that time had etched into her skin. "Stop," she protested. "I've...grown...old."

"No," he breathed. "Art perfect," he said, and his gentle words reassured her, even as the cacophony outside slid through the veil concealing them.

She dared to lean into his touch.

How many nights had she lain awake, aching for this?

The feel of his body against hers?

And now, here she was, precisely where she most wished to be, and she would not allow vanity to steal her moment. "I've missed you," she confessed, her hands lifting to trace the contours of his still-perfect face. "Not one day passed that I did not think of you."

His hand seized hers, dragging it down, pressing it against the beat of his heart. "Nor I you," he said, whispering her name again—an invocation, a prayer. He pulled her closer as though he could merge their bodies into one, and Gwendolyn reveled in the strength of him, and in the seclusion of this alcove, their embrace was fierce. Years of longing poured into every moment.

Even now, uncertain of what the next moment would bring, she clutched at the fabric of his tunic, terrified he might vanish if she dared release him.

"I feared I would never see you again," she whispered against his chest.

His arms tightened about her reassuringly. "And I you," he confessed. But then he chuckled, squeezing again, this time more gently. "Oh, but what an entrance you made!"

Gwendolyn laughed.

"Not a moment too soon!"

Beyond the alcove, the court was a boiling pot of bellows. The din beyond their sanctuary rose, voices of dissent reverberating even into the alcove, and Gwendolyn grimaced.

"I see time has not softened their disdain for me?"

It wasn't a question; the evidence was plain to see.

"We've faced insurmountable odds before," he said, kissing her forehead.

Gwendolyn smiled wanly. "Now what? It appears...we've sparked a new rebellion."

"Not I," he said with a bit of that old mordacity coloring his tone. But then he peered down at her, a perfectly wicked smile tugging at the corners of his beautiful lips.

"What are you thinking?" she whispered.

He did not hesitate. "I am thinking we should give them what they demand. Tonight, you will emerge from this alcove—no longer a queen of men, but my bride."

Gwendolyn's heart thudded, a wild, unsteady rhythm. "Now?!"

He regarded her, his eyes softening, though his jaw remained set. "Do you think waiting will make a difference?"

She shook her head, and something in his expression shifted—tenderness mixed with resolve, as though some long-held burden had slipped from his shoulders at last. "Let us seize this moment," he said, and squeezed her hand. "If you will have me?"

"I will!" The words left her lips before she could summon any protest. He caught her hand, swift and sure, and pulled her along behind him. Her pulse hammered against the cage of her ribs as they stepped out once more, into a sea of hostile faces.

Málik's steady presence at her side was a balm, lending her strength she hadn't realized she still possessed. But then, without warning, he lifted their joined hands. His voice rang out—clear, commanding, impossible to ignore.

"Behold! You asked for a queen! I present to you, Gwendolyn calon gadarn!"

Bold heart? She blinked at the sobriquet, then smiled,

even as the court erupted into a storm of protest. In the tumult, she caught sight of the young Fae noblewoman—the one whose mother had barred her way to the dais. The girl's eyes burned with venomous fury, her lips curling into a sneer. She glared at Gwendolyn for a long, simmering moment, then spun on her heel and bolted from the hall.

CHAPTER
FIVE

Mortified, Lirael fled the King's Hall.

She was so utterly furious tears would not come. But then, it was not her heart that had been summarily crushed—simply her pride.

She darted through the corridors, every step echoing her fury, her breath heavy with indignation as she wove her way through the labyrinthine palace.

All her years of careful planning reduced to this!

Her father's voice, persistent but distant, called to her, but she dared ignore him, hurrying her pace. Her silken gown, made to dazzle, now tore about her legs as her heels clicked against the old stone floor. She muttered an oath over the indignity of it all, and pressed forward, unswerving, until at last, she reached her private quarters, bursting inside, and slamming the door. Only then did she turn, her blue eyes glinting like blades against the half-light of her chamber.

She was incandescent with unspent rage as she waited for her father. But she didn't have to wait long. He opened the door without bothering to knock, his imposing figure silhouetted against the flickering light of the corridor. Knowing enough not to speak with the door open, she intended to wait for him to enter and close the door, but her blue eyes smoldered with rage, her ire equal to her confusion, and she couldn't wait. "He chose her *over* me?!"

For a moment, Lord Elric said nothing—no apologies, no reassurances—and her voice trembled with barely contained rage. "A mortal, father! She took what is mine!"

She knew Málik did not love her. But neither did she covet his love. She wanted the Horned Crown and the legacy it would bring. She wanted what her father wanted—to see their blood rule at last. She turned to pace; her torn skirts tangling about her legs. Her beautiful new dress was ruined —all the careful detailing lost in her hurried escape.

"How could you stand by and do nothing!" she whined, once again turning on her father.

Lord Elric's answering smile grew thin. Only Lirael ever dared take that tone with him—not even her mother dared. Their family had risen from the lowest echelons of Fae nobility through Lord Elric's cunning and patience. At last, he held sway with many of the highborn, including the ministers of the Shadow Court, whose patience with the mortal kingdom had long since waned. He was not a man to be tested, and despite that, she persisted.

"Why did you say nothing whilst that filthy beast stole my crown? You said those portals were closed? How is it possible for her to breach our realm so easily? How, father! I don't understand!"

Lord Elric stood considering, still saying nothing as he

stepped into Lirael's bower, then gently closed the door behind him. It sealed with a soft click. "Patience has never been your virtue," he said with a frown. "This...development...whilst most unexpected, is not unwelcome."

"How can you say such a thing?! *I* am supposed to be queen—*me*! Not her!"

"Do you believe I will allow carefully laid plans to be thwarted so easily, Lirael?"

Still petulant, she shook her head. "It's too late!" she contended. "He's already announced their betrothal. What can you do?" she asked.

Still, a flicker of hope had ignited within her at the familiar glint in her father's eyes. She knew him well. Already, he was weaving the threads of a new scheme.

"*She* is mortal. That will never satisfy the Court's demand for an heir. They will tolerate many things, Lirael, but not a mortal queen. That is a bridge too far."

Lirael's breath caught in her throat. "Do you mean to overthrow him?"

Lord Elric chuckled darkly, a sound that sent shivers even down his daughter's spine. "That would be...*inelegant*. No, Daughter. We will play the game with finesse, and once we are through, you will not only have your crown, but I will have my way with the mortal lands."

Lirael lifted the tail of her gown, wringing it into a knot as she listened.

"Your Dragon King is young and impulsive," he allowed. "His persistence with that mortal only proves as much." Lirael nodded, because a hundred years was like a day to her kindred. Against mortal years, Málik's age could hardly be construed as young, but he was certainly younger than Aengus Óg when Aengus took the throne. And meanwhile, her father and his ilk had been around since The Year of the Awakening. If he said the elders would never accept a mortal bride, it must be true. Lord Elric paced, his steps measured.

"The court will be divided," he said, scheming aloud. "We will use her arrival to our advantage. It will be the wedge we need to drive discord."

"But you cannot arrest her," Lirael said, and frowned, not entirely satisfied. "You saw what he did. He took her straight into Tech Duinn, and there shall keep her, as he has the Druids."

The king's private quarters had been doubly warded since Aengus' day. Once inside Tech Duinn, there was no one who could reach them who did not have Málik's permission to enter, and he had very loyal guards who would allow no one within an arm's length of his person.

This was why there had not yet been an attempt on his life, when half the Shadow Court's ministers disagreed with his *politiks*. Even those fool Druids were protected despite having objectors within the King's own circles. His rule was absolute, regardless of her father's machinations, and he had been working for years now to undermine Málik's authority, with little progress. And they had been so close to breaching Tech Duinn—so close. Once inside, Málik's days would have been numbered.

Lord Elric ceased pacing and turned to Lirael, his features tightening into a mask of determination. "I will begin with whispers in all the right ears," her father continued. "It will be simple to plant seeds of doubt about her true intentions."

He shrugged then. "Who can say for certain? Has she come for love, or does she seek to usurp this kingdom, as she did her poor, dear husband's?"

Lirael's brows twitched. "The one called Locrinus?" Even she had heard the tales of that cruel human beast. If anyone had deserved a blade to the heart, it would be him.

Her father ignored her. "I intend to remind the Fair Folk it was she who took Aengus' head—to what end? To steal a relic that should have been rightfully ours?"

Lirael thrilled at his words. "And what should I do?"

He grinned then, revealing a perfect row of porbeagle teeth, sharp as knife blades. "Quite simply, you challenge the mortal's lineage and her worthiness to stand as our queen."

Lirael's pale brows collided. "But...what will *that* do? Málik doesn't care, or he'd have sent her away."

"Think, Lirael," he urged. "The Fae Court has laws... ancient and binding. Not even a king may circumvent them..."

"The Rite of Blood," Lirael said, and her father nodded.

"Precisely, clever girl."

Lirael's eyes flashed with malicious satisfaction, following her father's plan.

The Rite of Blood was an archaic law, seldom used, but binding even so. Once a challenge was issued, Gwendolyn must prove her Fae lineage or forfeit any claim to the throne. However, she would not simply find herself excluded from wearing the Horned Crown, she would be imprisoned for the rest of her days, or banished to the mortal realm—and this time, the Shadow Court would invoke words to keep her from reentering. But there was a flaw in his plan...

"Málik is king...surely he——"

"Will have no choice but to comply," her father asserted. "Once invoked, the Rite must be satisfied. If he does not allow its due course, he will himself be found in contempt."

Lirael smiled, then frowned. Really, it would be a brilliant plan, except that she remembered the rumors about Gwendolyn's birth. It was bandied about that she was a changeling—stolen from the Fae and placed as a human child. If there was even a shred of truth in that, this could present a dangerous possibility. If Gwendolyn could prove her ancestral connection, however tenuous, the Rite of Blood would not work as they hoped. Such a revelation could even bolster her claim, tying her more firmly to Málik, and even placing herself above him. "What of Gwendolyn?"

"Rumors are not proof," he said, having expected her question. "Manifestation or blood is what the Rite demands." His eyes gleamed with dark amusement as he dismissed the idea with a wave of his hand. "Did you see a Fae queen when you looked at her?" He shook his head. "Not I!"

"So... even if she once had Fae blood, she may not be able to prove it?"

"Well," her father said, dissembling. "She *could*...but the burden of proof will lie with her," he said. "And she will not have any opportunity to confer with the elders until the trial convenes. Until then, she will find herself...detained."

Again, he smiled, and the sight of his grin gave even Lirael a shudder. "We all know how those trolls run that prison—a mortal could easily meet her demise. Moreover, that prison," he reminded her, "unlike Tech Duinn, is not warded."

That was true. It was why the Druids held court in their library, expecting even the trolls to attend them there—imagine anyone trying to educate those rude beasts. She wished a horde of *piskies* would gnaw off their toes—if one could find their toes amidst all that gnarly hair.

Lirael could barely contain her excitement now as she imagined the scene unfold—Gwendolyn, broken, chastened, as the court denounced her love as an abomination.

They would take her away in irons, and thereafter, Lirael would stand triumphant at Málik's side—or not, if he was dead—with the Horned Crown atop her head. "When do we begin?" she asked, delighted.

"Tonight," he said, his grin expanding. "I am not without manners," he suggested. "A welcome feast will be the perfect occasion...for an arrest."

Scarcely able to contain her glee, Lirael clapped—yet another party, and another pretty dress to be worn, only this time, it would end in her favor.

Curse that hideous mortal once and for all!

CHAPTER
SIX

Tech Duinn, they called it—the king's private sanctum, so named by the Fae Court and by Málik himself, after his own father. The House of the Dark One. It lay at the city's heart, a borough carved from black basalt and granite, a fortress within the palace, and a sanctuary besides. The name alone suggested a gloom to rival the City of Light itself, but there was nothing dark at all about the whitewashed halls of Tech Duinn. It was vast and splendid, with galleries and gardens, its walls rising stark and pale against the shadowed stone, protecting not only the king's quarters but a universe of wonders within.

And in those gardens—cool and shaded, far from the city's brightness—strange flowers bloomed, heedless of the sun or season. They thrived in the deep shadows where sunlight never touched, growing wild and beautiful in defiance of the world above.

It was like nothing Gwendolyn had ever seen.

But this was the oddest thing: During her first visit to the

City of Light, she'd had no chance to visit any location but the King's Hall; and there, only perforce. Yet this inner palace —these corridors and chambers—felt inexplicably familiar to her, the way it once felt to wield the Sword of Light.

It was an odd sensation, unsettling and yet... known. As though some part of her already belonged here, or had wandered these halls before. Strange, yes, but familiar all the same.

Much as Gwendolyn loathed to confess it, she had never truly felt at home in the palace at Trevena—not as a child, nor in all the years since. Little doubt it was her home—the only one she'd ever known—but she had so often blamed her mother for the awkwardness that clung to her there. Now, amid the hush and serenity of Tech Duinn, she felt an unmistakable sense of belonging. How strange, after all, that even knowing her Fae roots, she had not believed them until this very moment.

She realized then, all at once, how ill-suited she had been for the world of her upbringing. She had always been the outsider, even within her own walls, and she had spent so long searching for some fault in her mother as an explanation. But here, with only the soft light and the gentle quiet for company, there was no denying it—she belonged here. The sensation was at once foreign and familiar, as though her soul had always yearned for this and only now recognized it.

She wondered if, in some strange way, she had always known it, and if that was why the palace at Trevena had never felt quite right. Perhaps it was never her mother's fault, but simply the truth of her blood, and the truth of who she was.

She let the feeling settle over her, unsure whether to weep or to laugh. For the first time in her life, she felt as though she might finally understand herself.

Málik, walking at her side, remained silent and watchful, his presence as much a part of this netherworld palace as the bedrock from which it was formed. Occasionally, his hand brushed hers, but he did not guide her otherwise, seemingly content to allow the garden itself to do the work of seduction —and seduce her it did. As they walked along, Faerie Flames danced along the meandering paths—a thousand wisps of light flickering like candles in the wind, yet never extinguished.

Here and there, strange insects whirred, with wings that refracted the dim light; and in the deeper alcoves, Gwendolyn glimpsed faces—eyes blinking—from inside the knotty boles of unfamiliar trees.

"Korreds," Málik said, noting the direction of her gaze.

"What are they?"

"Fae," he said, shrugging. "Tiny, but shy. They traveled with us from Hyperborea. They bear the most remarkable knowledge of minerals and stone. It was their expertise that found us the adamantine—and, back in the day, when we occupied the mortal lands, it was they who located the copper so abundant throughout Cornwall."

Gwendolyn tilted him a glance. "So, we have the korreds to thank for our wheals?"

Málik gave her a nod and a half smile. "Something like

that. Although I'm certain they never meant to leave their work for your mortal-kind. In their world, they are better known as knockers. But that is *your* name for them, not *ours*."

Yours. Not ours. Gwendolyn bristled, bothered, although she didn't know precisely why. It wasn't so much his use of those words, *ours* and *yours*, but after her dubious welcome, she didn't relish that he, too, saw her as *other*. It was something she had not considered, even knowing she would have the Shadow Court to contend with. She simply never painted Málik with the same brush.

"This is...lovely," she said, shrugging it off as she swept a hand along an intricately carved stone balustrade, admiring the patterns inlaid.

Again, familiar though...not really.

Except...

Pausing, she traced the outline of a rune—a knot of lines that reminded her of the symbols embroidered on her mother's wedding gown.

"Wards," Málik offered, and she furrowed her brow.

"For protection," he explained. "Enchantments, if you will. Some installed by Balor, others by my father, and... Aengus." He glanced at her and sent her a playful wink. "They are like garlic to a *piskie.*"

"*Piskies* dislike garlic?"

He smiled. "Conclusively. Even more than trolls disdain *piskies.*"

"Well..." Gwendolyn said, laughing softly now. "That shows how much *I* know!"

Indeed, she thought. There was so much knowledge she

lacked—never once did it occur to her that those symbols could be magic. The tunic he had worn in the mortal lands was covered with the same runes, and yet, today, his robes were free of them.

His gaze followed hers to his vestments. "A gesture of faith," he explained. "For the event of my betrothal," he said, and Gwendolyn inhaled a sharp breath.

"Oh," she said, when she could speak beyond the knot in her throat. But now so much made sense—the young noble Fae who'd fled the hall, and the elder who'd barred her way.

"And then you arrived," he said, offering Gwendolyn another playful wink.

He had been so pleased to see her, but she wondered now if he regretted his decision to wed her. There was no doubt that their reunion had caused a bit of a stir. "I could go," she suggested, with a plaintive lilt to her voice.

His voice held a measure of humor. "We have gaols and I am not averse to using them," he said, letting the veiled threat dangle, as though testing to see how she would respond.

"But you wouldn't?"

"Or perhaps I would," he said with a smile, trying to sound serious, but Gwendolyn knew him too well. He would never resort to keeping her a prisoner. If ever he had been tempted to undermine her free will, he'd have spirited her away before her wedding to Loc. But he did not.

More's the pity.

"Alas," she said, though she had no regrets.

Really, she wasn't sad to know she had interrupted his

betrothal, and, in truth, thanked the Fates for intervening. How could she bear it to be stuck here, watching Málik with another woman—or another Fae? And that, too, was loathsome—knowing that she had lost him because *she* was no longer Fae. And then forced to remain whilst he built his life without her.

In truth, she had never once considered these things—only that he might not still love her as she loved him, never that he would have wed another. She imagined the awkward dinners, the silent glances exchanged over her head, voices whispering in languages she half understood but could never claim as her own. There was a lull in their conversation as they continued to stroll through the gardens.

Gwendolyn peered up to find him watching her, his eyes sparkling with a strange mixture of humor and regret. "You know I would not. Even so, you might come to think of Tech Duinn as your prison, Gwendolyn. These past years have been...a trial."

He exhaled wearily. "I have loyalists—men and women who would die to defend my rule. But much has changed since Esme's rebellion. She was Aengus' true heir, and some claim she left in protest of my ascension." He whispered it, as though the words themselves might turn to knives.

"But that is ludicrous," Gwendolyn said, grateful for the shift in topic, however slight. "We both know she doesn't want the crown." She almost smiled, remembering Esme's disdain for such things, but the memory soured before it could bloom.

He shrugged, a motion so small it might have been

mistaken for a shiver. "Ah, but she never said so—not exactly. And though we Fair Folk are blessed with many gifts —and you once accused me of knowing your mind—that is not among them. Her silence after the battle at the River Stour left many believing she had fled in protest."

Gwendolyn frowned, searching her memory. "Wasn't she the first to kneel when they crowned you?"

"Oh, she was," he agreed, his gaze going distant. "But now, there are some who question even that. I've heard it said she knelt out of grief, mourning the loss of her father's crown." He almost smiled, but there was no humor in it.

Gwendolyn snorted, unable to help herself. "Of course. Because that is precisely how Esme should respond to any slight. Gods, I have never seen her act with anything but forthrightness. If she wanted the crown, she would have made it known—loudly, and with no room for doubt."

He said nothing, but Gwendolyn could see the truth of it in the lines around his mouth. The silence that followed was heavy, but at least it was honest.

She lowered her gaze, worried, and for a long moment, neither of them spoke.

"Málik... what if your court refuses to accept me?"

"Our court," he corrected, and Gwendolyn shook her head.

She was pleased to hear him say so, but it was easy for him to say. It was not truly her court; it was his. Changeling though she might have been, now she was mortal—as breakable and blood-bound as Locrinus, doomed to bleed and die as easily as any other. No amount of wishing could make it otherwise.

Even Málik seemed uncertain, yet still he repeated, "Our court. You are my queen, even as I am your king, and they will learn to embrace you, or face my wrath."

Gwendolyn's heart fluttered at the steel in his voice—a threat, barely veiled, laced through every word.

It was a delicate reminder of who he was.

But he sighed again, the sound heavy, as though it pained him. "Alas, we all share the same malady. Our lives may be long, but our memories are as short as a mortal's. I know this, and you know this, but without Esme, it's our word against theirs."

Gwendolyn thought, not for the first time, how much simpler things might be if she could only shift her form, as the Púca did, and return herself to her former likeness.

"Alas... some of us have no memory at all—for certain things."

This was her greatest lament. She had no inkling of her former life, and today, of all days, Gwendolyn was reminded acutely of this. But if he understood her complaint, he gave no sign.

The silence between them stretched, and Gwendolyn wondered if he simply did not know what to say. She could not remember what she had lost, and that somehow made the absence of it all the more keen. It hurt, this not-knowing, this emptiness where her past should have been.

But she would not beg him for comfort.

Not now.

Instead, she turned her face away to hide the prick of tears.

Still, he said nothing.

And so, the moment passed, and Gwendolyn let it go.

Together, they continued to navigate the garden's winding paths.

"As you must know, Esme did not remain in Trevena," she offered. "She was gone with the portals." And now, though not for the first time, Gwendolyn wondered what business had taken her sister so far from everything she'd ever held dear—most notably Bryn, and the rebellion she'd waged so long. Gwendolyn had only assumed Esme had returned to the City of Light, but clearly she had not.

"I know," said Málik, perhaps misreading her tone. "But please do not worry; you'll be safe here until I can assign you a proper Shadow. As much as Aengus was despised, those wards served him well..." He fixed her with a long look, arching a brow. "Until you."

Gwendolyn stiffened at the implication, her lips thinning. "Well, I did not come to slay him," she protested. So much of this had never been discussed previously—mostly because she had never found the right moment to broach it. After returning from the Underlands, she and Málik spent the better part of their journey north at odds—until arriving in Skerrabra. Thereafter, only one thing had occupied everyone's mind...vanquishing Locrinus.

"I came prepared to bend the knee," she said.

Málik nodded. "There's no love lost betwixt my ilk and humankind. As generous as your proposal might have seemed—and it was—Aengus would not have accepted it, Gwendolyn."

"Pity," she allowed. "I would like to have known the great Poet King." A swarm of *piskies* flew past, offering a momentary distraction from the weight of her unspoken thoughts.

"So...the entire premises are warded?"

"Yes. The earliest construction of Tech Duinn was not so elaborate," he said. "Only a small bower where Balor could lay his head without fear of waking with a blade to his throat. It was my father who expanded the premises and the wards, and thereafter, Aengus, who made it so..."

"Glamorous?" Gwendolyn suggested.

He smiled. "Aha! You remember him," he said, and Gwendolyn had every sense that he meant it quite pointedly —as though she had known him very well in her former life, though she still could recall little—only that he was the reason she'd fled.

"So Balor was Nuada's successor?"

"Yes," said Málik, "But it should have been my father. After Nuada lost his hand, and the Shadow Court seduced Balor into betrayal, it was Balor who took the crown. My father—he plotted with Aengus to return the line of succession to its rightful course, but... something happened between them. Something changed. From that day, Aengus was never the same. When my father took the throne, Aengus plotted against him, weaving me into his schemes as well—a fact I perhaps regret, although I am uncertain I would have chosen my father's side, even if I could have."

"I see," said Gwendolyn, hungry for knowledge.

She knew only this much: Málik had been loyal to Aengus. Although if Esme was to be believed, it was not by choice. And now, Gwendolyn sensed there was more to the tale—layers of it, buried deep, perhaps even unknown to Málik himself.

"What put them at odds?" she asked.

Málik shrugged, a world-weary gesture. "I believe it had more to do with the balance of power than the circumstances of our exile, although that is the story told and retold."

She stared at him, waiting. "Explain."

He fixed her with a pointed look, as though measuring how much truth she could bear. "After the Ending Battle with the Sons of Míl, we did not come here to find the Underlands unoccupied. It was teeming with creatures, and none at peace. Trolls, spriggans, korreds—all vying for dominion. Our arrival turned the tide for the trolls."

"So the trolls are our allies?" she asked, uncertain, the words tasting strange on her tongue.

"Our?" he echoed, with a smile that was half shadow and half challenge, and for a moment, Gwendolyn couldn't find her answer.

"Most," he allowed, when she did not reply at once. "Not all. When we first arrived, we took up near the Lake of Fire. That Slemish area was predominantly theirs—hard won, so I am told. On the other hand, this area we are now settled in belonged to the Púcas—creatures friendlier to our plight."

"By plight, you mean the exile?" Gwendolyn asked.

Málik nodded, silent for a moment, as though measuring the weight of her question.

"Our decision to relocate returned the Slemish lands to the trolls. They wanted it—always have—and by then, we were all weary of the constant tremors."

"And the relocation was your father's suggestion?"

He hesitated, the pause stretching long enough that Gwendolyn wondered if he might not answer. But at last, he spoke. "No. My father never wished to leave the Lake of Fire, nor the adamantine to be mined there. He was the one who drove us from Hyperborea to seek the precious alloy— fevered, obsessed, he turned the whole of your mortal lands into a pit of mines, desperate to find the promised ore. In truth, it was a blessing for our kindred to be exiled, and to find it here."

Our, he'd said, and the word brought a smile to Gwendolyn's lips.

"It was Aengus who bartered the deal with the Púcas, offering them protection in return for this land." He exhaled, the sound drawn from deep within. "That is why I sided with Aengus over my father. I never condoned the taking of those lands. That was the root of all our troubles."

"What became of the Púcas?" she asked.

Málik shrugged, the gesture heavy with old sorrow. "A volatile illness ran its course—left the Púcas unable to shift form. That was their doom. One by one, they were hunted and slain by spriggans."

Gwendolyn looked up at him, brow arched. "And yet, you once told me spriggans did not exist?"

"I did." His mouth quirked, almost a smile, but not quite. "No doubt to placate you. But it wasn't a lie—spriggans were believed extinct. They haven't been seen here for millennia. Once the Púcas were gone, so were the spriggans. I do not know where Aengus found the army he sent to the Druid village."

A shiver ran through her at the memory—Devil's Walking Sticks, bristling with thorns, fierce and merciless. Not Fae, she thought, but something older, wilder—a race born of the world's primal bones. The thought of seeing one again made her skin crawl.

"So… what is her name?"

"Who?"

"*She* who would like to be queen?"

"Lirael," he said without feeling. "Silvershade. Her father is my High Lord Minister, and by now, I warrant he's taken his grievances to the Shadow Court."

"For his daughter's sake?"

"For his own. To be clear, if he could have wrested my throne for himself, he would have done it. He does not have so many confederates as he believes—merely enough to make my life difficult. His daughter was the only chance he had to gain support of both the Seelie and Unseelie Courts."

"Can he prevent us from wedding?"

Málik stopped abruptly, turning to face Gwendolyn, his expression sober. "No," he said. "As I've said, words are binding. Vows even more so. I've already declared my intention, and I meant it with every fiber of my being. There is no one but you, Gwendolyn. There has never been anyone but you, and I will love you equally in any form you bear." His hand lifted to her cheek. "I love you," he said, and put to rest any fear she had over his regrets. There was such heartfelt emotion swirling in the depths of his silver gaze. How could she ever doubt? Gwendolyn felt the warmth of Málik's palm against her cheek, and the world seemed to narrow, its focus sharpening to this single, intimate touch. His words, resonant with commitment, echoed within her, stirring a tempest of emotions she'd struggled to keep quiet. Her heart thumped wildly within her breast.

Málik smiled, a faint upturn of his lips that didn't quite reach his eyes. "There is only one way to end our union," he reassured. "It is to finish me...or you. This is why I must entreat you to remain within Tech Duinn...unless you are with me...or my guards."

The surrounding gardens suddenly seemed less enchanting. But her fingers sought Málik's, threading through them as though to anchor herself against the storm she sensed gathering. "I will be vigilant," she whispered, and he drew her close.

"My father warned me about your Shadow Court," she said. "He told me they would never accept a human and Fae union."

"It is true," he said. "But come!" And then he took her by the hand, pulling her along.

"Where are we going?" she asked. They'd been wandering for what felt like hours—too long for it to be mere leisure—and at first, Gwendolyn had thought he simply meant to show her the grounds, as one might a guest who'd only just arrived. But after all that had transpired since her arrival, and their conversation just now, she doubted he had time for idle strolls. "It's a surprise," he said.

A surprise? What sort of surprise could he possibly have prepared? There was no way he could have anticipated Gwendolyn's arrival—nothing in his manner in the hall suggested he'd known. Still, she trusted him, and so she followed without protest as he led her through the garden's end, through yet another door, and then into a maze of corridors where the air was thick with the scent of stone and the soft flutter of gossamer curtains, their edges stirring in some unseen breeze.

At last, he stopped before a tapestry—a moonlit forest, all silver and blue shadows—and, without warning, stepped straight into the woven scene, pulling Gwendolyn after him.

CHAPTER
SEVEN

G wendolyn gasped, breath catching in her throat, as the world shifted and she stood amidst a copse of silver birches, the ground dappled with morning light.

For a moment, she could only stare, dumbstruck, at the woods that surrounded her—so real, so vivid, she half expected to hear the distant call of a Cornish dove. It was as though she had been sent back to the tranquil wilds of eastern Cornwall.

Her hand trembled as she reached for the nearest tree, fingertips grazing the bark. It was cool, and rough, and utterly indistinguishable from the birch woods she remembered as a child—before the blood, before the loss, before the wedding that was a massacre.

"How is this possible?" she whispered as she stood there, uncertain, heart pounding, unwilling to move for fear that the vision might shatter.

But the woods did not fade. The trees remained, and the morning light crept over her skin, gentle as a mother's touch.

Málik's eyes glinted with mirth. "Regrettably, it is only a glamour—an illusion. Like that time you believed I'd turned you into a tree."

Yes. That.

Gwendolyn remembered, and the memory made her shudder, because that day had nearly been her last. Locrinus' men had been so close in pursuit—so close she could still feel the frantic thudding of her heart as she'd darted through the trees, desperate to escape. She'd nearly been recaptured, and if not for Málik's intervention, she would have been. Even now, the recollection of those moments left her weak at the knees.

"But this feels so real," she said, her voice barely more than a whisper as she turned in a slow circle, taking in the beauty of their surroundings.

He gestured to the tapestry. "Every thread—every color—holds some echo of the living world. The memory of sunlight, the scent of moss, the hush of wind. That is what you see, and why it seems so real."

"It's beautiful," she whispered.

He watched her with a crooked, fang-toothed smile, linking both hands behind his back, evidently pleased with her reaction. "This grove exists in the natural world—somewhere near Bodmin, if you must know."

"Bodmin," Gwendolyn whispered, a fresh wave of homesickness washing over her, although she knew that wasn't Málik's intention. Those moors had been one of her favorite places to ride—wild and windswept, where she could forget the weight of her crown and simply be.

"Alas, Bodmin, too, has changed, though I miss it," she said, nostalgia tightening her voice as she reached out again, this time to study the leaves. "There's a part of me that feels...torn," she confessed, her eyes sparkling with unshed tears. She wished to be here—truly. Yet she couldn't ignore the grief she felt over having left Habren and Bryn behind—and, really, everything she had built.

Málik's features softened as he closed the distance between them. "I understand," he murmured, reaching to brush away a tear that traced the curve of her cheek. "The bond between land and sovereign is not so easily severed... not by time, nor by distance."

Gwendolyn shook her head, wiping another tear with the back of her hand. "It's not simply the land," she insisted, her voice raw.

He hesitated as though weighing his words, and his gaze lingered on her, gentle, searching. "No," he agreed quietly. "It never is."

With a flourish of Málik's hand, the forest transformed into an unfamiliar glade where golden poplars loomed and silver flowers bloomed bright against the twilight.

"This one mayhap not so bittersweet...Hyperborea," he said. "But I doubt you remember." He watched her face closely, and Gwendolyn shook her head.

"What of this one?" he asked, waving his hand yet again, grinning as crystalline water cascaded from somewhere into a clear, beautiful pond.

"Porth Pool?" Gwendolyn whispered with awe.

He nodded. "Before the Rot, and, truly, before Trevena was itself a glimmer in your father's eye."

Gwendolyn turned up the palms of her hands. She could actually *feel* the cool droplets as they splashed her arms and face. "Here, the line between illusion and reality is...like a waking dream," he suggested as she bent to disturb the water, watching as ripples spread from her fingertips.

"So you can create anything?"

"Within reason," he allowed, moving behind her as she stood again, and his presence made her pulse quicken. "Alas, even here, certain truths remain immutable. Death. Love..."

His hands settled atop Gwendolyn's shoulders, and she dared to lean back against him, closing her eyes—it had been, oh, so long. "If the location within is altered, does this reflect upon the tapestry as well?" she inquired as his arms encircled her waist.

"Clever. But no. Those tapestries are more like portals than windows. They remain as they were, displaying only what they were woven to portray—a moment frozen in time, regardless of what transpires within." He kissed her neck. "These are all Arachne's creations."

"*Arachne?*" One fang grazed gently at her flesh.

"Oh, yes...the Orb Weaver's Cloak is the least of her mastery."

Absentmindedly, Gwendolyn's fingers lifted to the fabric of her cloak, the memory of Arachne and her grotto flashing vividly through her mind as Málik's voice took on a seductive quality. "You see, her skills were essential in creating the Veil that separates our worlds."

"The Féth Fíada?" Gwendolyn guessed, though she could

hardly focus—Málik's lips grazed the hollow of her throat, his words melting into her flesh as she leaned back, surrendering to his embrace.

"Yes," he breathed, the word barely more than a whisper, hot against her skin. "If you can imagine... that Veil..." Another kiss, softer this time, just below her ear. "...simply a tear in the fabric of the world..." His breath stirred the fine hairs at her nape, and Gwendolyn shivered, unable to help herself. Oh, but this was a history lesson she could thoroughly enjoy—far preferable to any she'd endured at the hands of the mesters. She tried to concentrate, to follow the thread of his explanation, but his touch was unrelenting, and her mind swam with sensation. "A tear... in the world?" she managed, her voice unsteady.

Málik's lips curled into a smile against her skin. "Precisely." His hand traced her arm, slowly and deliberately, giving pleasure with his fingertips alone.

Gwendolyn's thoughts scattered, unable to muster a single clever retort. She could only tilt her head, granting him better access, her breath coming sharper with every word, every kiss.

And if this was the manner in which he meant to instruct her, she would gladly forget every lesson but his. "As for Arachne," he went on, "it wasn't until many moons into Aengus' reign that she was banished to her lair." He paused, letting the words settle, then added, "For her part in your vanishing."

"And how did you feel about my... vanishing?"

"I know you did it to protect those you love," he said softly. "But knowing that hardly eases the pain of what was lost—especially since I believed *I* was your one-true love."

Gwendolyn's heart constricted at the raw vulnerability in his voice. Without hesitation, she turned and lifted a hand to his cheek, tracing the sharp angle of his jaw. "You are," she whispered.

She was here, was she not? She'd given up so much—everything, to be sure. There was no going back, not now, not ever.

He took a step closer, his voice raw, as though he'd swallowed broken glass. "I searched for you across realms, through time itself." There was no mistaking the pain in his words. "Every beat of my heart in your absence felt as though it would hasten my end." He reached up then, brushing his thumb across the plane of her cheek, and said, "Promise me you'll stay."

Spoken so, it was no command, only a plea, and Gwendolyn's heart squeezed at the sound of it, though she tried not to let it show.

Of course, she would stay—of course she would. Why would he believe otherwise? He needn't even jest about keeping her imprisoned, nor fear she would ever leave him when she had so willingly abandoned everything only to see him again.

Responding to his need—hers as well—Gwendolyn reached for him, daring to embrace him, wrapping her arms about his waist and holding him close. "I am sorry," she murmured. "I only wish..."

He doubled his arms about her, resting his chin atop her

head. "I know what you wish," he said as he kissed her. "I wish it too...but your memories will return in time."

Just so, they stood so long as Gwendolyn once again inhaled his magnificent male scent.

This too gave her a sense of belonging she couldn't explain.

It gave her a sense of...*home.*

"I've missed you," she said huskily, and his arms tightened about her possessively, his lips moving to her neck. A gentle scrape of his fangs sent a delicious shiver down Gwendolyn's spine, and a soft, involuntary moan escaped her as she melted into his arms, her fingers curling, clutching at the fabric of his tunic.

He kissed her, and she returned his kiss with equal fervor, feeling his heartbeat even through the weight of his tunic—a steady rhythm that echoed her own quickening pulse.

For the moment, the world about them faded, leaving only the two of them entwined in this magical forest. Her fingers sought and found his beautiful hair, taking pleasure in its silken texture.

"I have long dreamt of this reunion," he murmured, his voice husky with desire. "Alas...now is not the time. More than anything," he said. "I would love to have you to myself... but there is something I wish to show you. Come," he demanded. "Before I lay you down and ravage you like a mindless beast."

Once more, his hand found hers, his fingers tangling with hers as he pulled her through the greenwood. Until suddenly...the trees vanished, revealing a clearing bathed in light as silvery as his hair.

At the center stood a turreted construction, and the sight of it stole Gwendolyn's breath. She gasped aloud, and made to halt, but Málik tightened his grip upon her hand, dragging her along, leading her *into* the building, where all the trees were replaced by towering shelves stretching impossibly high...They were filled with books, and once again, Gwendolyn gasped with delight. In all her life, she had never seen so many tomes—and none like these. Not rolled. They were flat and bound.

Málik pressed lightly on the small of her back, urging her forward.

"This is the Máistirs' library," he explained. "Where the Knowledge of Ages resides. Every breath every creature ever took has been recorded within these tomes. Indeed, the life of every blade of grass, the death of every star. Here, you will find answers to your questions...if only you know the right question to ask."

Gwendolyn's fingers longed to reach out and touch *every* manuscript! To feel the weight of so many centuries right there in her hands. "Everything?" she whispered, her voice soft with wonder.

Málik nodded, a crooked smile playing at his lips as he watched her. "It is a repository of everything that has ever been, all that is, and all that will ever be. The Library of Rhakotis was modeled after it."

Gwendolyn spun to face him, realizing only belatedly. "But you called it the Máistirs' library? Does that mean...?"

He nodded, and precisely as he did so, out from the aisles came both Emrys and Amergin, arguing like perfect old fools.

"Emrys!" Gwendolyn exclaimed and ran to him. She collided with him, and he gave her an "Oof!"—returning her embrace, laughing so joyfully that Gwendolyn could feel his fat belly quake between them. "They've fed you too well," she said, jesting, and Amergin laughed as well, slapping his ample belly before embracing her too.

"Welcome," said Amergin, greeting her. "It has been too long since last we saw you."

"Neither of you has aged one day!" Gwendolyn said jealously. "I can scarcely believe you are here!"

"Where else would we be?" asked Emrys.

Indeed, where else? Gwendolyn had known they'd gone to retire in the City of Light. Still, she wondered why they were *here*—in Tech Duinn, in *this* library.

Málik stood back, watching the three of them together, his expression delighted. After a moment, he said, "I trust the lot of you have much to discuss. May I leave for a while?"

This, he asked of Gwendolyn, and though she was surprised, she nodded. "You will be safe here," he added. "As I've said, the entire premises has been warded. There is no entry without authorization."

"Yes, certainly," Gwendolyn said as he came forward, placing a hand to her cheek, leaning in for the briefest, sweetest of kisses, and then lingering a moment too long.

He whispered for her ears alone. "As you can well imagine, I have matters to attend," he said with regret. "But worry not, my love. I leave you in excellent hands." He spun then, dropping the hand at his side as he addressed the Druids.

"May I impose upon you to return her to my chambers in two bells' time?"

The Druids nodded, and Málik gave Gwendolyn one last glance, then turned on his heels, and strode away, vanishing into the belly of the archive.

"Well," she said, turning her attention to the Máistirs. "I suppose we have much to speak of?"

Emrys cleared his throat, his deep-set eyes twinkling brightly. "Indeed, we do, *Banríon*. There is so much you will need to know to prosper here, and much we hope to learn from you."

"In fact," said Amergin, "I believe you are late."

"Or just in time," argued Emrys.

Gwendolyn furrowed her brow. "How could either of you have ever imagined I would come at all if the portals were closed?"

Amergin winked at her. "Love always finds a way," he declared.

CHAPTER
EIGHT

The Druids were eager to recount all that had transpired since abandoning the mortal lands. Gwendolyn listened intently. She knew Emrys better than Amergin, but both had stood beside her against Locrinus, and both had lent their influence to win her grandfather's favor. They were her allies once, and now, in the Underlands, they would be again. Amergin had already dwelt among the Fae, so his return was almost expected, as though he belonged here more than anywhere else. But Emrys—Emrys had a brother he left behind, and Gwendolyn could sense the ache in him, the way it hollowed out his voice when he spoke. Although he tried to hide it, Gwendolyn saw the cost etched on his face. She understood it, that loss—how it gnawed at the soul. Gwendolyn heard the sorrow and the longing for what had been left behind. No one crossed into the Underlands without leaving something precious behind, but he seemed happy enough, as eager as Amergin to share his stories.

No doubt, Gwendolyn understood the sacrifices he had made, but if their purpose here was any indication of it, their decision had been for the best. Working together, they'd found a shared purpose in creating an academy for the trolls, who'd proven surprisingly eager pupils.

Apparently, the trolls had taken to their studies with enthusiasm. Gwendolyn nodded along. Though, truly, she could hardly imagine any troll doing aught but ripping things in twain or belching.

"Their progress has been most remarkable," crowed Emrys, his careworn hands folding into the sleeves of his gray robe. "Yestereve, Yavo plotted the trajectory required to hurl a boulder through our practice targets. Impressive indeed, though we'd hoped he would apply that knowledge to somewhat less destructive pursuits." A smile touched Gwendolyn's lips.

The image of trolls bent over their lessons struck her as... incongruous. She tried to picture them hunched over their desks, with faces scrunched in concentration, but could not. She had only ever thought of them as witless, lawless creatures.

And no matter. If the Druids claimed success with them, who was she to doubt?

They also saw fit to enlighten her about Lirael and Lord Elric's long-held quest to see his daughter seated upon the throne. Some months ago, he had inspired the Shadow Court to issue an ultimatum to Málik that he should wed. He had planned to announce the betrothal at the celebration she'd interrupted.

"Were you at the gala?" Gwendolyn asked, wondering if they'd witnessed the affair.

Emrys shook his head.

"We were not invited to the gala," Amergin said. "It was the Púca who told us."

"I have not yet seen the Púca," Gwendolyn complained.

"He comes and goes," said Amergin.

"Alas," complained Emrys. "We've not left Tech Duinn for more than two score years—ever since I took a blade to the back."

"Oh, no!"

He turned to show Gwendolyn his wound, lifting his tunic, revealing a bare arse, and Gwendolyn flushed, even as she searched for the injury. She found it beneath his lowest rib, a scar that was unmistakably intended to impale the reins...but someone did a poor job. Clearly, they did not have Málik as a teacher.

"Drat!" she said.

"Drat, indeed," grumbled Emrys. "You might think so long as they put up with this one—" He gestured toward Amergin. "They might have welcomed me eagerly."

"Well, I do not bore them," suggested Amergin, and Emrys shot him a baleful glare, lowering his tunic and covering his arse. "At any rate," said Emrys. "They failed; and here I remain!"

"Thank the gods," Gwendolyn said.

"Or someone, mayhap not the gods," suggested Amergin. "I do not believe he engendered their support either."

Emrys furrowed his wiry brow. "I only met the one!" he contended.

"And she scorned you," Amergin said with a knowing smile that crinkled the corners of his old blue eyes. Gwendolyn watched the exchange with curiosity. These two, confined to their sanctum for more than two decades, had developed the rhythm of some who were wed.

"At any rate," said Emrys. "Thereafter, Málik ensconced us here, certain our lives were at risk."

"Particularly of late," said Amergin darkly. "The Shadow Court has grown quite bold. So I've been told, at Lord Elric's urging, they would like to reclaim the Druid villages, and oust our brethren."

"Gods! No! What of Lir?" asked Gwendolyn. "Have you heard from him?"

Emrys' eyes slanted sadly. "Not even once. After the portals were decommissioned, there was nothing for it but to trust they are well." He sighed. "However, I am assured that all who remain Betwixt are hidden from both realms—no one can harm them in that place. And really, of all Fae, only Málik has the means to cross the Veil, and he will not—not even to visit the village."

"He gave his word," said Amergin soberly.

Gwendolyn furrowed her brow.

So Málik had the means to cross the Veil, but did not?

Then again, she never gave him a reason to return, so she could not blame him when he did not.

"What can you tell us of the mortal lands?"

"How does Trevena fare?"

"What of the Rot?"

"How go the tribes?"

The Druids' questions came rapid fire, and Gwendolyn's

smile warmed as she considered her son. "My boy—Loc's son—" She shrugged. "Sits upon my throne—his throne now. I gifted him my Kingslayer and left Claímh Solais as I found it when I came to this realm—embedded to the hilt in a stone near Trevena. Someday, someone worthy will find it and reclaim it, I am certain."

The Druids both nodded soberly.

The Sword of Light, she understood, had its own purpose. It was never hers to keep, only to borrow. It belonged not to the Fae, nor to Kings simply for the wearing of a crown. Indeed, if there ever came a peasant with the heart of a king, it would ignite for a just cause. Its magic was ancient—older perhaps than the Fae themselves, its legacy one of justice, meant to empower those with the heart to wield it.

There was no wonder it was not her father's to wield.

He was not The One.

"As for the Rot...once our people were reunited, it took little time for the Rot to correct itself—but my beloved Porth Pool never revived and the *piskies* never returned."

"Of course now, and we know why," said Amergin, tugging at his beard. "I do not believe magic will ever return to the mortal lands."

"What of Trevena?" pressed Emrys.

Gwendolyn lifted a shoulder. "The city fares well enough, but the port brings fewer and fewer merchants by the day." She sighed. "But at least there is peace—for now."

"Oh! And the Temple of the Dead has been completed at long last. The neighboring tribes send their priests to study, even as the *dawnsio* has revived. My mother is so pleased."

"How does Queen Eseld fare?"

"Happily wed," Gwendolyn revealed.

"Caradoc?"

Gwendolyn nodded.

"What of Baugh?"

"Gone, so I am told. He left Albanactus with the thane-dom, and of course, while *that one* is far less offensive than his brother, Loc, he renamed the entire north after himself!"

"Alba," said Amergin, testing the name as, once again, he tugged at his beard.

Gwendolyn nodded.

"Such hubris," said Emrys. He then added, "One can only hope Loc's son will not follow in his father's boots." Gwendolyn shook her head adamantly, her gaze softening at the mention of her boy—no longer a boy, in truth. "I worry more he will not find himself a worthy bride—someone who will complete him. Habren is everything a mother could ever hope for, and I worry about him, though I trust Bryn will guide him well, and Taryn will keep him safe."

"Taryn?!" asked Emrys. "His Shadow?"

Gwendolyn nodded.

"A woman?!"

"How...democratic," remarked Amergin.

"No more so than to kneel before a queen," suggested Gwendolyn with a smile.

"Well, that is true," said Amergin. "But you know history will scheme to negate your legacy? They will build statues to Corineus, and even to Gogmagog, but never you."

Gwendolyn shrugged. "I do not need statues," she avowed. She was more than certain they spoke true, but she could hardly worry now about what people years from today might do. "It matters not, dear friend. *We* know the truth, and as it should be, there will arise no good king to any throne who will not have the help of a good woman. This is *our* way—to support and nurture."

She smiled wistfully. "Would that it could be different, and maybe someday?"

Emrys nodded solemnly, and Amergin did as well.

Just so, they carried on and on, speaking at length as though nary a day had passed between them. It was as though, in fact, they were as they once were, because without a mirror to peer into, Gwendolyn could too easily believe no time had passed, when neither of these two old souls had aged a day since she saw them last.

Nearly two hours later, they were still chatting, now examining tomes.

"That one is quite extraordinary," said Emrys, looking particularly satisfied that Gwendolyn had chosen it without his guidance. "It conforms to the reader," he explained.

Amergin hurried to add, "It will tell you what you most wish to know—if it deems you worthy to know it." He reached out, daring to finger it, brushing the cover, and Gwendolyn watched as the words on the vellum shifted, forming intricate patterns. It was quite unlike the rest of the tomes, bearing a cover made of a shimmering material that Gwendolyn did not recognize.

"Dragon scales," Amergin supplied, noting her expression.

"From the last of the Great Wyrms," said Emrys, his voice carrying a note of reverence.

"Wyrms?" Málik had once referred to his father that way, and to himself as well. But Gwendolyn did not understand what it meant.

"The Ollphéisteanna," explained Amergin. "Shapeshifters, to be sure. "Some are given to the oceans, some to the mountains, and others to the sky. The greatest among them was Caoránach, the mother of all Great Wyrms of Éire."

"How does this relate to Málik?"

"His father is the Wyrm's son," Emrys interjected.

"The tome was created by artisans who understood some knowledge requires...shall we say, sacrifice?" He exchanged a meaningful glance with Amergin before continuing. "This dragon—Caoránach—gave her scales...willingly."

The words hung in the air between them, weighted with implications that Gwendolyn could not fully grasp. "When you—or, that is to say, your former self—left Tír na nÓg, she gave the tome to her grandson...to be read on the event of his ascension."

"Málik's grandmother?"

Emrys nodded.

"Is she...?"

"Dead?" He nodded again. "Oh, yes."

Gods. The act spoke of a love so profound it made Gwendolyn's chest ache. "Why?"

"No one can say for certain," said Amergin. "But, so they tell me, she was banished to the depths of Loch Dearg, and when she tried to make an escape, it is said she carved the course of the River Sionainn as she slid towards the sea. There is speculation she was en route to see Manannán mac

Lir, and that he himself took the book from her to keep it safe. Once the portals were closed, Manannán gave it to Málik, although what it conveyed to him, no one knows. The truth betwixt those pages is revealed only when the secrets are most needed."

"So his grandmother wrote the book and my father knew of it?"

Both Druids nodded fervently.

Gwendolyn frowned. Though it wasn't so much that she was upset by the disclosure. She already knew Manannán had kept things from her, but the revelation left her with even more questions. Clearly, Málik knew about the book, and he wanted her to read it.

"We should like to know what it says to you, but now we are short of time," said Amergin before chastising Emrys. "This one can never hush his mouth! And now we've wasted too much time. *He* said, two bells before we should return you, and we've only moments to comply!"

In fact, there was no true censure in Amergin's tone; it was clear these two old men had become close, teasing one another as easily as brothers...or lovers?

Whatever the case, Gwendolyn was pleased to note it, because she knew Emrys must be missing Lir—and, as for Lir, she hoped he, too, had found himself a bit of joy amidst his Druid brothers.

"Bring it," demanded Emrys. And then, with a very concerned tilt of his head, he said, "Do you remember which tapestry you came through so you can return?"

Gwendolyn nodded, and Emrys crooked his finger, begging her to follow. "There is another way to exit this library, as Málik did earlier. But it leads straight into the Shadow Court. We are much safer exiting the way you came," he explained and then led her from the library, into the forest, and through the tapestry, then through a long, winding corridor.

"There are locations in that library that remain accessible to the court. There is a lobby for the elders to submit requests for tomes, and we have been tasked with their keeping."

"This is not Málik's most popular decision," added Amergin. "But, as there have been many attempts to steal or manipulate the texts for personal gain, he felt it necessary."

"The written word is both a treasure and a weapon," added Emrys. "Only depending on whose hands will hold it. But Málik also knows that knowledge must never be withheld. Hence, the elders have a concession to request certain tomes...under certain conditions—without gaining access to the library itself. However, there is an enchantment on that book," he said. "It can never be spoken of aloud, and this is why I was so pleased that you found it on your own. We worried about how best to present it."

Gwendolyn listened as they strode, and finally, they reached a set of large, unwieldy oaken doors. On their approach, those doors flew wide, and Emrys gestured for her to step inside, but did not follow.

CHAPTER
NINE

"Won't you join me?" Gwendolyn entreated.

"Oh, nay!" returned Emrys. "That...is...your private quarters."

"Of course," Gwendolyn allowed, disappointed, though she supposed he was right. It was just that one glance within apprised her that Málik had not yet returned, and she did not relish the thought of being alone in this still strange place, even with the wards for protection, although at least she had the book.

"We should leave you to your studies," suggested Amergin as Gwendolyn stepped into the chamber, clutching the dragon-scaled book to her breast.

"I will see you again, yes?"

"As often as you please," said both Druids at once, and Gwendolyn smiled, for they spoke as one.

"Do not pore over that too long," suggested Amergin, raising a finger. "I am told there is to be a feast in your honor this evening."

Gwendolyn furrowed her brow. "A feast?"

She saw no one approach the Máistirs' library, and Málik did not reveal any such thing before he left. However, that library was enormous, and it was possible that during one of their forays down the aisles, Amergin or Emrys was approached by a messenger.

"Indeed," he said. "This evening."

"Will you attend?"

Both men shook their heads, and Gwendolyn nodded, understanding.

And with all that needed to be said now said, both her friends departed with a rustle of robes, and Gwendolyn found herself alone in the king's bower, with the dragon-scale tome heavy in her arms.

Once inside, the heavy door closed with a soft click, and she stood for a long moment, allowing her eyes to adjust to the soft light of the room. But this chamber was grander than any she had ever occupied, even as the Queen of Cornwall.

Indeed, Cornwall's palace was remarkable enough, but the floors were in places still dirt, and the walls were mostly bare, except for the Great Hall and the King's Apartments.

Here, nearly every wall was adorned with tapestries, and the furnishings seemed to have grown from the stone itself —except for the bed. And that—if one could call such an ethereal creation a bed—appeared to float above the floor, suspended by nothing at all. The frame, crafted of twisting silver branches, stretched toward a rounded ceiling. Gossamer curtains hung from the canopy, shimmering with an opalescent sheen that reminded Gwendolyn of silver-threaded spider silk—more of Arachne's weaving? She approached the bed, setting the dragon-scaled tome down upon a coffer at the foot, then peered about, taking measure of the space that was presumably now hers.

At one end of the chamber stood a steaming bath—awaiting her? Vapor rose from its interior, and it carried the fragrance of exotic oils and herbs, not unlike those her mother had once favored. However, there was another scent here...something deeper and more primal—a scent that reminded her of Málik himself.

At the other end of the room stood a wardrobe crafted of the same silvered wood as the bed, its doors slightly ajar to reveal garments within—brightly colored silks and soft velvets in jewel tones that caught the light like liquid gems.

Gwendolyn moved toward it, and like the room's doors, the wardrobe flew wide as though eager for her to examine the contents—and so she did.

The gowns—all unlike anything she had ever worn—were every one more exquisite than the former. Her fingers traced rich fabrics that seemed to breathe beneath her touch, some cool as a *winterbourne* stream, others warm as a summer afternoon. She couldn't help but remember all the lovely, shimmering materials that graced those dancers' forms on her first visit to the City of Light—attire that defied description. One woman had worn a gown that released a flurry of glowing petals that floated delicately to the floor, creating a carpet of light in her wake. Her partner had summoned a breeze that lifted all those petals into the air, compelling them to swirl about them like a maelstrom. Another Fae had worn an outfit crafted from delicate crystals and strands of pure light. And another, with a cloak of cascading water that never touched the ground...

One dress in the wardrobe drew her attention most definitively, and she took it from the wardrobe, shook it out, and carried it to the bed, laying it down.

It was a masterpiece of craftsmanship, interwoven with threads of silver that caught the light. But, as beautiful as it was, it was the book that most drew her curiosity, so she sat beside the dress, lifting the tome from the coffer, and turned it to the first page...

The words scrambled to form a single cohesive sentence. It read: "On the celebration of the wedding of Diarmuid and Curcog..."

Blinking, as though shedding a lifelong haze from her memory, Gwendolyn recognized her true name, and then... she remembered Málik's true name as well.

CHAPTER
TEN

They were married.

   As Curcog and Diarmuid.

   Here lay the proof...written in what Gwendolyn knew intuitively to be blood.

His grandmother's...

Her fingers tested the ink that neither smeared nor faded under her touch; it was immutable, eternal. How many times had she dreamt of encountering some tangible fragment of her past, some undeniable evidence of the life she once shared with Málik? And now, here it was—in vibrant clarity.

Her trembling fingers traced the ancient script, and with every word she read, fragments of her memory stirred like flickering embers coaxed from dying coals.

Every moment of their nuptials lay detailed within the enchanted tome—painstakingly detailed by a creature who had clearly loved them both. The words flowed soulfully, and through them, Gwendolyn felt the rush of days long gone...

Married by the Goddess Danu in a ceremony under a mantle of stars that shone brightly even under the bright light of day. This was her wedding, Gwendolyn thought, and in her moment of acceptance, something unimaginable occurred...

Recollection washed over her like a tide against Cornwall's shores—suddenly, violently, and completely. And then the words on the page became visions outright, spilling from the tome into the room where she sat, transforming the entire chamber, and ushering Gwendolyn to another place and time...She watched with wonder as the celebration unfolded, every detail a brushstroke on the canvas of her life. Vows made near a placid blue lake near a vast field of blooming daisies, and this was as real to her now as though she stood amidst it all.

She could *smell* the flowers.

Hear the sweet notes of a harp.

Feel the warmth of the sun.

The bride wore a blue gown with wide-flowing sleeves.

Beside her stood Diarmuid in a silver-blue tunic, smiling down at a face that was hers as she'd once spied it in an Underland pool—a sharp-toothed, pointy-eared countenance she was once startled to glimpse—her true form, not the mortal shell she'd worn so many years.

Golden hair cascaded down her back, and her eyes... were the same storm-gray. A golden circlet atop her brow caught the light of the stars, and Gwendolyn's breath hitched as she watched her younger self—her true self— reach for Diarmuid's hand. Their fingers intertwined with such familiarity that her own hand quivered with the memory of it. That couple, whose faces were bright with love, exchanged torcs, and as they stood before a company of Fae—many familiar—a chorus of voices rose in song.

Later, after the ceremony, victuals were served upon long tables, including an array of fare almost too lovely to eat, every dish a vibrant display.

Her memories returned in a wild torrent as the revelry surged; laughter mingled with music, dancing, and children rushing by with tarts in hand. But...it was so unlike Gwendolyn's wedding to Loc that it overwhelmed her, and she closed the book, a bittersweet taste filling her mouth...

Like dandelion greens and regret.

For all the years lost.

For trading *this* for what she'd ultimately received.

Locrinus, with his cold, cruel heart!

The vision faded as swiftly as it had appeared, leaving Gwendolyn alone in the chamber, her eyes stinging with unshed tears. More than anything, she longed to make this her home, but considering the dubious welcome she'd received, she knew her place would not be so easily won.

Did she think she could simply reclaim her true self?

One look at her would prove her a liar. The Fae would see only what she had become—a forgotten soul disguised by mortal flesh.

But now was not the time to pine over what was lost. She had a feast to attend, and the last thing she intended to do was arrive looking disheveled and unprepared. She wanted more than anything to make Málik proud, and to be the mate he deserved.

Rising from the bed, she set aside the book and moved to the steaming bath, determined to win the court's trust...or at least their respect.

CHAPTER
ELEVEN

Dressed and waiting, Gwendolyn paced the king's chamber, the hem of her gown swirling furiously about her ankles. Every passing moment heightened her anticipation of the evening to come. Intuitively, she understood the feast was no simple gathering, nor, in truth, a welcome. She had little doubt Málik intended it to solidify her position as his bride, and yet, despite the return of her memories, she was not Curcog; she was still Gwendolyn.

Again, she stopped before the mirror—a polished obsidian stone that reflected her image with terrifying perfection. No pointy ears, no porbeagle teeth.

And yet...something in her bearing *had* shifted.

The way she held her shoulders?

The tilt of her chin?

The glint of knowing in her eyes?

She was both Gwendolyn and Curcog at once...both warriors in their own right, and tonight she would leverage both to fight for what was hers—not wielding a sword as she had once done upon the battlefield, but rather, with her presence and poise.

Who, if anyone, would champion her cause?

Málik, she knew, but he was only one against so many, and if the Shadow Court mutinied against him, where would that leave them both?

Worrying her lip, she lamented the marked absence of fangs as she inspected the gown she had chosen. It fit as though it had been tailored to her form, hugging her every curve and falling in elegant, graceful folds that shimmered with every movement. Her hair, arranged in intricate braids, was interwoven with tiny silver beads that caught the light. The image she presented was every bit the queen, so why did she feel an impostor—a child, once more, only hoping for her mother's nod of approval?

Deep breaths did little to calm her racing heart.

Turning from the mirror, she heard the knock on the door, and froze.

Málik would hardly knock, would he?

Steeling her nerves, Gwendolyn moved hesitantly toward the door, her heart skipping a beat as she pulled it open. It was not Málik.

There stood two guards.

One taller and more imposing, stepped forward, bowing his head slightly. "The feast awaits, my queen," he announced with formality, his voice echoing in the spacious chamber.

"Where is...the king?"

"We've been tasked with delivering you," said the guard.

Why did he make it sound as though she were meant to be served, not a guest of honor?

The guards waited, silent and unmoving, clad in what she presumed was Málik's own livery—a deep, midnight green, almost black in the torchlight. Each man gripped a spear, its haft wrapped in the glimmer of dragon-scale, and their watchful eyes glinted beneath the fanged shadows of their dragon helms. Gwendolyn trusted they were allies, not foes, only because Málik had said so himself: No soul could enter Tech Duinn without his express leave. It was impossible, he'd sworn, and she believed him.

Her heart tangled itself into knots as she moved to retrieve her cloak, the one she'd chosen for the evening. Her hands trembled, but she flung it about her shoulders with practiced grace. It hardly mattered whether Málik was at her side, she told herself. He had given his word, and here, in this place, his word was law.

Gwendolyn lifted her chin, nodded once to the guards, and followed them from the chamber, her every step measured and deliberate. She would not falter, not here, not now.

This was her court as much as it was his!

Wasn't that what he'd said?

Wasn't this what the book revealed?

The certainty of it settled over her as inexorably as the cloak of thorns she'd chosen to wear—a garment as wickedly lovely as it was cruel, every needle-point digging into her flesh.

The fabric itself was blood red with intricate black embroidery resembling thorny vines, and black pearl thorns that glinted against the torchlight. Given the choice between that and another softer, less punitive garment, Gwendolyn had chosen the cloak deliberately, not only because the wardrobe produced it, but because it was a thing of dark beauty, matched only by its cruelty.

Everything in this court was that way—even its denizens—beautiful and vicious.

If Gwendolyn must endure pain, let it be of her own choosing. And yet only as the weight of it bore down upon her and the thorns pressed into her shoulders, did she fully grasp the lesson the cloak meant to convey: she must be stronger, more unyielding, than her fragile human form suggested. She drew the cloak tighter, feeling every sharp sting, and set her jaw, certain that this was her time to prove she belonged. She would not be cowed.

She would not allow pain to defeat her. If she must bleed, so be it—she would bleed and endure, and let them see her do it.

She would outlast them all.

Stand tall.

Back straight.

Face them with courage, Gwendolyn demanded of herself as the guards, in their gleaming gold armor, led her through the maze of corridors.

She had never been one for elaborate gowns or finery—nor jewels for that matter—preferring instead the practicality of her battle leathers. Yet tonight, she understood: the impression she made would be as vital as any weapon in her arsenal. She needed to be seen—not as an afterthought, nor as a mere consort, but as the king's equal, his chosen partner, and his queen.

Queen Eseld had impressed this lesson upon her from the cradle: to be a queen, one must first be perceived as a queen. Her mother had known it by instinct, and though Gwendolyn herself had not truly stepped into Queen Eseld's shoes, she took her example from that young Prydein princess who had come, so long ago, to be her father's bride.

To win Cornwall, Gwendolyn had needed her sword. But to win the Fae, she must embody the regality she'd never fully embraced.

Tonight, she would.

The dress was a marvel—deep emerald silk, masterfully wrought, every inch alive with silver embroidery so intricate that the threads caught the light, setting the whole gown aglow with a shimmer of elegance. It put Gwendolyn in mind of a midnight forest: subtle, yes, but quietly rich, self-assured in its simplicity. The bodice plunged daringly, lending the dress a boldness that was neither vulgar nor desperate, but regal, as though daring any soul to challenge the right of its wearer to rule. It was not merely a queen's dress; it was a declaration, a standard unfurled for all to see.

Both gown and cloak swept the stone floors behind her, trailing like rivers of silk.

Past ornate doors and beneath arches of ancient stone that whispered of royal secrets, the guards ushered her forward. Until at long last, they neared the Feast Hall.

Two immense doors appeared before her, so tall and wide, it seemed they should admit giants. Each bore a dragon, slumbering, etched into the wood with such skill that the creatures appeared to draw breath, their sinuous bodies curled across the panels. In the wavering torchlight, the dragons' scales shimmered, catching every flicker and throwing it back in dazzling, shifting patterns—so lifelike that, for a moment, she half-expected them to yawn and unfurl, stretching claws and wings in the gloom.

Inexplicably, Gwendolyn's nerves settled at the sight, and she smiled.

Her mother had been so keen to unite the "dragon banners," thinking the dragon would be Loc. It was Málik all along...and this, at last, was the fulfillment of her prophecy.

The sound of music and laughter drifted towards them as the guards rushed ahead, shoving open the heavy doors, and Gwendolyn was momentarily blinded by the light of a thousand Faerie Flames.

Head high.

Chin up, she told herself.

Once more, she smoothed the folds of her gown—her heart fluttering like a trapped sparrow—and drew in a sharp breath, forcing herself to remember who she was. Not merely Gwendolyn of Cornwall, Queen of Men, but the Fae king's bride.

Wasn't that what the tome revealed?

Not that it mattered, not here, not now, with her pulse hammering in her ears and her hands trembling as she stilled the fabric. She must not falter.

She straightened her back, fingers lingering at her waist, and let the surety of the words in the dragon-scaled book settle over her like a mantle.

One last time, she gathered herself, smoothing the gown

until every pleat lay perfectly, and lifted her chin. Whatever awaited her in the hall, she would face it as the true queen—and as the Fae king's bride.

Giving a nod to her guards, Gwendolyn marched into the Hall with all the quiet authority she could muster. The hall fell silent at once, and a sea of faces, familiar and foreign, turned to gawp—some mayhap with curiosity, others with thinly veiled suspicion, still others with overt contempt.

The shift from revelry to stillness felt like the tightening of a noose, but, armored in her gown and cloak, Gwendolyn met their gazes with unflinching resolve.

She straightened her shoulders as she sought Málik and found him seated at the High Table.

Their eyes met and held.

And then he gifted her with a smile that stole her breath—a smile so filled with love and longing that it made her knees falter. He stood then, his every gesture measured as he descended from the dais to greet her, neither his gaze nor his smile wavering.

They met below the dais, and he extended his hand, his fingers brushing hers with a gentleness that sent a quiver down her spine. "You are...resplendent," he said, his gaze inspecting the emerald silk...and then lower...to the valley between her breasts—a liberty he had never dared.

Indeed, Gwendolyn had worn nothing so daring in all her life, and she thrilled at his attention. The pale-blue flames in his eyes ignited an answering heat deep within her.

For the longest moment, they stood in silence, and then he lifted his gaze to her shoulders, admiring the cloak.

He stepped back then, and the crooked smile that turned

his lips gave Gwendolyn's heart a flutter. For a moment, she couldn't speak or breathe.

The King's Hall, with so many watchful eyes, dissolved into shadow. There was only Málik and Gwendolyn...and the warmth of his hand still clasping hers.

The intensity of his gaze held her transfixed.

"You chose well," he whispered. "The gown suits you."

Her gaze fixed upon a golden locket he wore about his neck...a reliquary the likes of which some priests wore in the Temple of the Dead. Gwendolyn had never noticed it previously, but it was impossible to miss now. It gleamed as though newly polished, and noting the direction of her gaze, he smiled once more, and reached out, taking her by the hand, kissing it tenderly, before bowing, and if there was a message intended in his actions, it was this: Gwendolyn must be honored.

By the king, no less.

The gesture was lost to none.

He then captured her arm, looping it with his, before escorting her up the stairs. And once upon the dais, he led her straight to the King's Table, offering her the conspicuously vacant seat by his side. But before Gwendolyn could seat herself, he raised his voice to address the assembled.

"Lords and ladies," he began, his tone commanding silence.

With his free hand, he lifted, then raised his goblet. "A toast to *our* queen," he demanded, and, as Gwendolyn watched, every hand lifted along the length of every table.

With a tremulous hand, she found and lifted hers as well, the cool silver trembling against her palm.

"All Hail the Queen!" declared a few.

Others followed with mumbled praise.

It was *something*, at least—even if their commends were given grudgingly. But Gwendolyn could feel every pair of narrowed eyes, even as she did the thorns beneath her cloak.

It was going to be a long night...

Once everyone had drunk, Gwendolyn stole a sip of the sweet, heady wine, and was wholly unprepared for the taste of it. Like stars exploding, a burst of flavor ignited upon her tongue—rich and complex, unlike any wine she had ever tasted. Its warmth spread swiftly through her, and she felt a strange mix of exhilaration and calm. Hadn't someone once warned her—Lir, perhaps—that mortals should never eat or drink Fae fare? But this was pleasant, not unlike Hob cake. Another sip sent more heat creeping through her veins, along with an abiding tranquility that softened the edges of her anxiety.

And now, despite that the court's attention remained fixed upon her—all those thinly veiled smiles—she met them with a steady gaze. "To me!" she dared say aloud, and hiccupped.

Beside her, Málik chuckled as, one by one, more toasts were followed by the clinking of goblets and eventually, the hall returned to its normal ambience and the harp resumed as well.

Feeling less stressed, Gwendolyn took her seat, wondering why he had not sent her a pint of that wine while leaving her to dress.

All was well.

She was well.

But why shouldn't she be with Málik at her side?

As the feast unfolded, Gwendolyn allowed herself to relax into the evening. Peering about the room, she took in the lavish decorations and the bountiful feast laid out, and hiccupped again.

"I believe you've had enough...for now," Málik said with a gleam in his eyes. Reaching out, he slid the goblet from her fingers, setting it down.

Gwendolyn's cheeks burned, but nothing could diminish her smile—not even the sight of Lirael Silvershade seated beside her bird-beaked mother.

"I would ask what's in that," she said, laughing. "But I expect you to reply with the same maddening ambiguity as you did over Hob cake!"

She hiccupped again, and Málik chortled again, his laughter like music to Gwendolyn's ears.

"That," he explained, "is one of the finest vintages from the Eternal Vigne—the vineyard of Zeus himself. Fit only for such an occasion." He whispered low now, "It graces *every* table this eve. But take care. Its magic is subtle but potent."

"Too potent for mortals?" Gwendolyn dared to ask, a tinge of melancholy tainting her mirth. Still, her smile returned when Málik reached out to brush a stray curl from her face, then kissed her cheek.

"All you need ever remember," he said softly, "is that you are as much of this world as you are of Cornwall." His tone was light, but his eyes were sober.

"My arrival has unsettled so many. Emrys showed me what they did to him."

He lifted a brow. "Showed you?"

Gwendolyn lifted her shoulder, nodding. "He also said they have not left Tech Duinn for years. Until the guards arrived, I feared this might also be my fate."

"They *will* learn to embrace you," Málik reassured, and Gwendolyn sighed.

Despite the return of her memory, she could hardly expect anyone to accept her so readily, and neither could she tell them all she knew—not even Málik realized as yet.

This moment didn't feel like the proper time to speak of such a revelation—not with a thousand eyes trained upon them. So, with a breath drawn deep, she steadied herself against the inevitable trials of the evening and attempted to enjoy the feast. It wasn't difficult, especially with the help of the wine.

Forsooth. It was difficult not to find *some* joy when her senses were assaulted by a cavalcade of tastes and scents. Every dish that passed beneath her nose was more enticing than the last, and despite her earlier reservations, she sampled a few bites. The flavors were exquisite.

Throughout the evening, Málik remained attentive, his hand finding hers beneath the table—a far different partner at this table than she had known before.

Indeed, during their previous time together, she could only recall one occasion they had shared plates, or even dined at the same table—in her uncle's house. There, for the very first time, Gwendolyn had wondered what sort of partner he would be...and even dared wonder how the Fae made love—a titillating lesson she'd learned for herself whilst in the Druid village.

The Fae were *magnificent* lovers—very well-endowed and

deliciously corporeal, but there was a fusion of body and spirit that heightened every sensation. Even now, Gwendolyn found herself eager for another...reunion, and a blush warmed her cheeks.

Catching her gaze, Málik gave her a knowing smile.

Meanwhile, beneath the table, he squeezed her hand.

That's how they spent the evening...with playful exchanges.

As the feasting dwindled, the music softened, turning the "night sky" above into a velvet darkness, pin-pricked with starlight so that the entire Hall shimmered. Every so often, Málik leaned in, his words meant for her ears alone—a private jest, or some sly observation.

"That one," he murmured, tilting his chin toward a willowy Fae with hair like spun gold, "is Lady Síofra. She once challenged me to a duel to the death over a slight to her nose."

Gwendolyn's lips twitched. "Did you?"

"Slight her nose?" His mouth curved, dark with mischief. "I may have," he confessed, eyes alight. "I think I suggested it preceded her into rooms by a full breath."

Laughter bubbled up from Gwendolyn's belly—a sound she had not made in far too long. It startled her how easily it came.

"She is someone you should know. I warrant she'll be your dearest friend," he said, and then he looked her over, then again at Lady Síofra, who lifted her glass in greeting, her smile genuine and bright.

Málik watched her. "A divination?" she asked, but he only shrugged.

"I simply wondered if you had any memory of her," he said, and Gwendolyn glanced again at the noble Fae, who smiled once more, as though she already knew something Gwendolyn did not.

Gwendolyn shook her head.

Clearly, not *all* her memories had returned, and a veil of disappointment shrouded the evening. Thereafter, she studied the courtiers—every one—trying to discern who would be friend, and who would be foe. Repeatedly, her gaze returned to Lirael Silvershade, whose bright eyes were colder than a winter storm as she sat watching the dais.

Foe, she thought.

Decidedly foe.

In truth, Gwendolyn did not doubt for an instant that if she crossed paths with Lirael in some unlit corridor, the woman would not hesitate to run her through. There was a certain coldness about her—something that sent a shiver down Gwendolyn's spine, and brought to mind Loc's mistress, Estrildis. Estrildis, who had once delighted in Gwendolyn's pain, and tortured her for endless months in Loegria.

Even now, as Gwendolyn recalled that time, the memory of it clung to her skin like a bruise that would never fade.

But this time, it was Gwendolyn in a position of honor, and she would not cow to Lirael's disdain. Every line on the girl's beautiful face, every scoff concealed poorly behind a sip of wine, and each whisper she shared with her mother and father was perhaps a broadcast of hostility meant for Gwendolyn to perceive. But the new queen of this Fae Court wouldn't succumb to intimidation.

Not tonight.

She endeavored to ignore the girl as more servers appeared, bearing even more trays laden with delicacies the likes of which Gwendolyn had never seen—bright-colored fruits and pastries that puffed steam like miniature volcanos. Her curiosity piqued, she selected a small bite of fruit from the passing tray as an elder Fae leaned about to speak around her partner, presenting a question to Gwendolyn.

"Tell me...Gwendolyn...how do you find Tír na nÓg?"

Startled at first to be addressed so openly, Gwendolyn blinked, peering up at Málik to find his eyes mercurial—saying nothing, only observing.

A test?

"Quite lovely!" Gwendolyn replied.

The Fae woman's eyes glinted with amusement—at Gwendolyn's expense?

Indeed.

Her lips curled into a sneer. "Of course," she agreed. "*Your* home must seem quite dull in comparison." It wasn't a question, nor was it intended to be polite. Her meaning was lost to none, but Gwendolyn knew better than to speak in defense of her mortal lands—not here, not now.

She also knew that angering these creatures would never serve her in the end, so she searched for precisely the right response. Lifting her chin, she allowed, "I would argue each realm possesses its own splendor," she said diplomatically. "But *this* is now my home."

The woman said nothing, and Gwendolyn glanced up at Málik to find amusement dancing in his *icebourne* eyes. "Well played," he said low.

A tenuous smile played at the corners of Gwendolyn's mouth. "I learned to spar from the best," she allowed, then whispered, "Esme" lest he assume the compliment for himself.

He laughed, and Gwendolyn reached for his thigh beneath the table, squeezing gently—but, oh, the feel, so... hard...sent her pulse skittering. It was not quite what she intended or expected, but again, the familiarity between them was lost to none.

"Careful," he teased. "You will tempt a beast..."

The air between them sizzled with promise, and Gwendolyn's breath caught.

"Perhaps that is my intent," she whispered, and gave him a playful wink.

No longer was she the same innocent who'd once trembled over the thought of placing her virgin lips to the same goblet his lips had touched—nay, indeed.

Moreover...she had been too long without a lover—without him, and she had no intention of ever wasting another moment. Emboldened by the wine, she slid back her hand and said. "I am quite famished..." And she was, but not for food. Somehow, as it was the first time she'd visited this place, hunger was not a thing to be borne. Food was consumed only for pleasure.

A low rumble bubbled from Málik's chest, and a slow smile spread across his face.

Gwendolyn recognized the look of desire and thrilled.

"Perhaps we should retire?" he murmured for her ears alone, his voice thick with lust, and Gwendolyn squirmed in her seat. Briefly, she considered kissing him here and now, but the moment was thwarted.

"Majesty," interjected yet another courtier, this time addressing Málik, "Won't you regale us with the tale of how you and Lady Gwendolyn first met?"

As his partner had, the Fae lord had not used Gwendolyn's title—neither her new one, nor old—but, by now, she was accustomed to such insults. There was a time not too long past that her own people had been reluctant to address her as sovereign, despite that she'd earned it.

"It must be quite the story...to tempt a mortal into our hall."

This lord bared his porbeagle teeth, and a hush fell over the room.

The music faded, the air suddenly sharpened as Lirael Silvershade rose from her seat, raking her chair back, seizing the opportunity.

Tall and lithe, draped in a gown of midnight blue, the girl's eyes glittered with barely concealed malice. Her gaze fixed upon Gwendolyn as she addressed the dais, and now, having captured everyone's attention, she raised her goblet belatedly.

"Yes, Majesty," she purred, her voice dripping with false dulcet. "Please do...regale us...How did you come to meet your sweet mortal bride?"

Gwendolyn felt it, the prickle of a thousand eyes, cold and bright and hungry, waiting for her to falter.

But this was Málik's story to tell, not hers.

She wondered for a moment if he would answer—if he would tell them some sweet tale simply to placate them, or if he would seize the moment to assert his authority, to define their narrative in terms that none could question. Or even if he might reveal the truth of their bond.

But that was not what they wanted to hear. He knew, as she knew, they wanted a spectacle. They wanted to see Gwendolyn squirm. And so she braced herself, as she always did, for whatever would come next.

Beside her, Málik's eyes burned with an unseen fire, surveying the hall—every courtier, every attendant—before returning to the expectant face of Lirael Silvershade.

TWELVE

N ow it begins.

All night, I have watched the High Lord Minister's viperous tongue drip poison through my court—every word laced with dissent and betrayal. The taste of his duplicity is bitter on my tongue, and I curse beneath my breath as his daughter—his lovely, loathsome minion—abandons her seat.

At my side, Gwendolyn tenses, the line of her jaw taut as a drawn bowstring, but there is only so much I can do to shield her. This court must not perceive my affection as weakness. The choices I make tonight will dictate whether she is fated to live out her days sequestered with the Druids, or as a free member of this court.

So much as I love her—so much as I long to hold her close—I will not keep her prisoner, nor will I watch her die with a knife pressed to the reins.

No, tonight must mark a change, for better or for worse.

Gwendolyn's fingers tighten about my thigh, but the

gesture is not flirtatious. I find her hand beneath the table, and squeeze, a silent promise that whatever storms may break tonight, my commitment to her is unyielding.

And then, I turn to catch Lirael's eye.

She approaches the dais with practiced grace, her every step a performance.

Of course, it is.

This is what that harpy was bred to do—what a vision she is, too, a would-be queen worthy of the Fae, a beautiful nightmare in twilight hues. Her gown shimmers like midnight rain, every clap of her heel a warning of the storm to come. She is the very embodiment of elegance and deadly intention.

Behind her, Lord Elric watches with the patience of a spider who has at last felt the tremor of prey in his web.

"My king," Lirael says, spinning with her goblet in hand —her inflection on the word *my* so pointed it could draw blood.

I brace myself for a dose of her father's poison. It comes, as I knew it would, her voice sour as bitter grapes. "Esteemed members of our court—" The word *our*, too, is stressed, accompanied by a baleful glance toward Gwendolyn. "I stand before you now to address a matter of import."

A growl rumbles in my chest. "What matter so urgent it weighs upon you to interrupt my queen's feast?" I will not allow her to seize the moment. I know my words may seem cruel, when only hours ago Lirael had hoped to become my bride, but I need her to understand the finality of my decision...

Gwendolyn will be queen.

Gwendolyn is my love.

Lirael is not.

"A matter of law," she replies coolly, her eyes glittering as she turns to face the courtiers, not me, and I recognize the malice veiled beneath her siren's lilt.

Across the hall, the attendees shift in their seats as she pauses, milking the silence for all it's worth.

"I mean to invoke the Rite of Blood," she announces, her words hanging in the air like a drawn blade—a challenge, unmistakable. I know this law—an archaic convention from times past. But if even one of my Shadow Court supports it, I will be bound to its demands.

"The presence of a mortal at our King's table, whilst... charming—" She says the word with false affection. "Threatens the surety of our realm..."

Anger smolders in my gut.

Gods know. If I speak—if I rise—I will rip the tongue from her mouth and consume it myself.

I reach for my goblet—not to lift it, but to steady myself. My grip tightens upon the stem, the metal cold beneath my fingertips as her voice, icily calm, continues, every word coached by her father.

"Did we not agree to keep our lands separate?" she says. "How can we be sure there will not arrive... more?"

Mortals.

Since the Ending Battle with the sons of Míl, my kindred have blamed humankind for their banishment to the Underlands. To be sure, Amergin had a hand in that judgment, but it was my father who gave him the power to decide. Most of the denizens of my court remember... but not Lirael. She's a youngling compared to most. Not yet born when we were exiled from mortal lands, she has, no doubt, heard those tales from her father.

Her gaze sweeps the hall, blue eyes alight with a mix of righteousness and disdain. Her words themselves were a poison—not deadly, but sowing doubt and fear. With brows drawn together as though she were a guileless philosopher pondering the mysteries of life, she asks, "Please tell us... what assurances have we now that her kind will not overrun this city? How do we preserve our sovereignty?"

A murmur of agreement ripples throughout the crowd, and I feel Gwendolyn's grip tighten on my leg—a silent plea for support, or perhaps a brace against this storm.

I long to speak, but do not.

Lirael has already presented her challenge.

Nothing I can do or say will change the course of that. But if I murder her where she stands... there will be a new rebellion, forged by the groundswell of her blood.

The hall swells with nods and murmurs, and an undercurrent of unrest ripples throughout.

"Furthermore," she continues, emboldened now, her voice gathering strength with her purpose. "The law is clear..." Her bright blue eyes shine with triumph. "Even if these things are found to be without merit... only one of our blood may stand as queen. It is not simply a matter of choice or tradition. It is the law, which sustains us. You may choose to wed a commoner..." Her voice drips with malice, and her eyes gleam. "But you will not choose a mortal bride!"

Collectively, a gasp sweeps the hall.

Every eye in the hall shifts toward me.

No one has ever spoken to me so insolently in front of my court—not even Esme. Yet Lirael's audacity does not surprise me. Her father's voice speaks through her, and bitterness coats my tongue as I realize how deeply Lord Elric's betrayal runs.

At my side, Gwendolyn remains stoic, her eyes fixed upon Lirael, her face a mask of calm despite the turmoil I sense within her. But Lirael's disputation, directed at me, is the perfect excuse to intervene, and I rise, my voice slicing through the whispers like a blade. "You dare apprise me of what I may or may not do?"

Lirael shrugs. "Not I," she says coyly. "The law."

Silence settles over the assembly like a death shroud. But though hers is an affront that cannot go unanswered, my response must be measured. "You speak too easily of laws forgotten before you were a pup in your cradle," I say, a wave of fury rising from my entrails.

Gwendolyn's fingers pinch my leathers.

There is so much I would have told her if I could. But as Manannán is bound, so too am I. I can speak no words that will unveil our past, and if she cannot do so, then I am bound to silence.

My eyes flash with warning, but Lirael remains undaunted. Her posture straightens, indignation clear in her tone. "Ancient or not, those laws remain binding, do they not?" Her chin lifts. "My age matters not when our laws are written upon the stones from which this realm was built." And then she adds, with a glance at Lord Elric, "Anyway, my father is far older than you..."

I grin, but there should be no comfort in the jagged

presentation of my porbeagle teeth. "So... your father—" I flick a glance at Lord Elric. "Will challenge me now?"

The coward will never. He is a neophyte—a long-to-be king. His hand never once turned a blade, nor can he force his will beyond the councils. His place is in the shadows. He would rule through his daughter, and without the means to compel me, a challenge to me is a death knell.

"Lirael!" he admonishes. "Enough!"

Too little.

Too late.

My attention shifts to Lord Elric. "You seem to have forgotten that I am the law of this land! I will forgive your impertinence... because I know... your wound is fresh? But I advise you to weigh your words carefully." My question is directed at both, but my gaze remains fixed on Lord Elric's.

Beside him, Lirael's eyes dart about the hall—seeking allies, or perhaps gauging the depths of her folly. And yet, though her father's voice may have halted her tirade, the ember of her cause glows hot within her eyes. "Well," she says now, again lifting her goblet, dangling it between two fingers. "I propose," she says too innocently. "That we allow your lover to decide. If the rumors be true, she needn't fear. She needs but reveal herself here and now—and behold! If she cannot, she should be banished from this hall and this realm, never to return, on pain of death!" She spins to ask the nobles. "What say you all?"

Again, the court holds its breath, awaiting my response, and I am torn...

Between love and duty.

I cannot afford to alienate my court and keep the peace.

But neither will I entertain or accept challenges from Silver-shade's poppet—or rescind my promise to Gwendolyn.

Neither will I allow her to be abused by the whims of this court.

With deliberate slowness, I set down my goblet. "You tread on perilous ground here, Young Dryad. Your mother should have advised you better... jealousy is unbecoming."

The girl's eyes flash over my rebuke, but she quickly composes herself, a too-sweet smile spreading across her features. "Oh, I assure you, it has naught to do with jealousy. I speak out of concern for this court and its... welfare."

"Alas, the youngling speaks true," muttered an aged Fae with silver hair, his voice spurring yet another torrent of whispers. Lord Maelon, one of the oldest, most respected members of the Shadow Court. His support of Lirael's challenge makes my blood run cold because if he backs her, others will follow.

Indeed, his endorsement may even sway those who would otherwise remain neutral or side with me. Lirael's confidence grows, and she presses on. "If she is Niamh, let her prove it. Now, here, under everyone's scrutiny, and then we shall forgo the Rite of Blood."

"No," I say firmly. "Gwendolyn will not be subjected to petty tests!"

"She must!" Lord Maelon declares, standing, and the hall erupts into chaos.

"The Rite of Blood has been invoked!" says another minister, and one by one, each of the twelve Unseelie ministers arises from their seats, and their intention cannot be mistaken. The last to stand is Lord Elric himself. His obsidian eyes gleam with barely suppressed glee.

"Majesty," he begins, inclining his head. "Whilst we acknowledge your authority, we must still uphold the law, ancient though it may be. My daughter, no matter her reasons, speaks true." He clears his throat. "A mortal queen poses... shall we say, challenges?"

"I will not be defied," I say firmly. Then I gesture to the crowd at large, pointing toward each minister. "Every one of you old fools swore fealty to me, and, unlike my father, I will hold you to your oaths."

Lord Elric's voice is smooth as silk but sharp as a blade. "Yes, Majesty. But please know, it is out of our shared loyalty that we must insist upon upholding this sacred law." His obsidian eyes glint as he continues, "You, too, swore an oath when we lent you our armies to aid your... mortal queen. You gave us your word that you would separate our realms, and forsake all those lands held—including its queen."

My jaw clenches as I fight to control the rage building inside me.

"You dare speak of oaths? I have upheld my end of our bargain. The portals remain closed!"

"And yet," he counters, "Here stands a mortal in our hall, claiming the title of queen—our queen. One would argue this violates the spirit, if not the letter, of our bargain." He stands tall and proud, his eyes sharp and calculating. The game of Queen's Chess he began when he approached my dais earlier this day is now in full play and in view of all—a battle not of arms but wits, intended to trap me between duty and love, laws and promises. He knows I must abide by the court's laws—no matter how ancient or ill-conceived they might be. And knowing that, the taste of fear appears on my tongue, a bitter reminder of the stakes at hand. Despite my irritation and anger, I know any wrong move on my part will seal Gwendolyn's fate. The hall falls into a heavy silence, the tension palpable as every member of the court weighs the gravity of Lord Elric's accusations and my gaze sweeps the gathered Fae.

"Surely, My King, you of all, must understand the gravity of this predicament?"

Gods damn him.

I cannot argue with his point.

When I remain silent, Lirael's eyes glitter with triumph, and she turns to Gwendolyn. "The test is simple, my lady. You must only prove your Fae blood."

At last, Gwendolyn speaks, but there is no fear in her voice. She asks carefully, "How does one prove one's Fae blood?"

Lirael's features twist into a sneer. "The answer is so simple, even a cretin mortal should be able to understand. You open a vein, you bleed," she snarls. "As for the proof of one's lineage..." She sneers. "Only one of our ilk can mend a wound cut by the ceremonial blade."

My beautiful, brave queen now rises, squaring her shoulders, her mettle showing at long last. "In my time, I have faced tyrants far greater than you, Mistress Lirael. Whatever your trials, I will face them."

Whatever it was I hoped she would say, this is not it.

"Gwendolyn," I whisper. "You needn't agree to this. I will find another way."

"There is no other way," she says beneath her breath. "I know, and you know it as well as I. To be sure, they must be satisfied I am worthy to be your queen... and I *know* I am," she declares.

Then again, "I know who I am."

Her eyes beg me to trust her, and I do. But my jaw clenches, a muscle twitching beneath my skin. I relent and sit down. "Very well." My voice rings cold and clear as the caution within it. "A challenge has been issued and accepted. May it not be said I stood in the way of justice."

Lord Elric nods, all pretense of concern wiped from his visage, and a rush of excitement flitters through the assembly, followed by another sluice of furious whispers.

He steps forward. "Very good," he says, his voice carrying a trace of ill-concealed malice. "This trial shall be held on the morrow. May the gods bear witness to her test." From beneath his robe he draws a set of iron shackles, advancing upon Gwendolyn. "Now you must surrender yourself to the court."

"No!" I rise again, stepping in front of Gwendolyn. "You overstep, Silvershade! Your queen will not be treated like a common thief!"

"It is only tradition, Majesty," he reassures, his voice gentle. "Any who face the Rite must surrender to the custody of the court until they are proven innocent."

"No," I say again. "The only place my bride will be sequestered this eve is within the confines of our chambers." I snap my fingers to summon my guards, and before anyone can object or intercede, I seize Gwendolyn by the hand, then lead her from the hall, through the alcove, with my most loyal guards at our back.

Gods be damned! The Fae Court is as fickle as the seasons. Allegiances turn with the wind. But these few have bound their lives to mine by blood and bone. They will die before allowing any harm to befall their king or his queen. The moment we are through, I whirl on Gwendolyn, my composure shattering like ice against a spring thaw. "What the bloody hell were you thinking?" My hands find her shoulders, gripping too tightly. "You know not what you've agreed to!"

"All will be fine," she argues.

"Nay, Gwendolyn," I say, my voice raw with anguish as I touch a finger to her sweet, beautiful face. "The Rite is a rite of blood!" I pause, searching for words that might convey the magnitude of what she faces. "It is left to their discretion whence that blood should be drawn."

When she still does not understand, I explain, "They will put the dagger to your heart, and not even Fae magic will heal that wound quickly enough! But if they had taken you now, there would have been no trial on the morrow!" My voice catches, and I turn away, unable to meet the storm in her gray eyes as she realizes for the first time the magnitude of the invitation she has accepted.

I pull her into my arms and hold her because the challenge has been issued and met, and there is nothing I can do but watch my beloved die.

THIRTEEN

Málik's bare feet padded furiously against the stone floor. Half-dressed, tunic discarded—or rather, hurled across the bedchamber—and his breeches haphazardly unlaced, he radiated a restlessness that Gwendolyn had never witnessed in him before. Not even on the eve of battle.

Moreover...they had been far more intimate than this, and far less dressed, but there was something innately vulnerable about him now, a temper that bespoke the depth of his love for her and the breadth of his terror over what his Shadow Court might now do. He looked like a cornered creature—wild and threatened, still frighteningly powerful.

I am safe now; she wished to say, but she didn't believe it would assuage him at the moment, nor would he believe it when there were Shadow Guards begging entrance to Tech Duinn.

"Málik," she whispered, intending to go to him, to soothe him. She rose from the edge of the bed where she'd been sitting, her feet touching the cool stone floor, but before she could reach him, he spun about, eyes blustering like a storm-laden sky.

"They will not be merciful!" he said.

I am not worried; Gwendolyn longed to say, but she did not, because she could see his consternation, and did not wish to dismiss his concerns. "Did you expect she would do such a thing?"

"No!" he said, turning to pace again. "I did not! Though should have!"

He was getting angrier by the moment, but it was difficult to say at whom, because his voice carried a measure of self-contempt with no small amount of regret.

"That girl has always been...so ambitious—her parents even more so. Her mother once offered me her body for the promise of her daughter."

Gwendolyn grimaced over the notion—a mother bedding a daughter's intended? "That is...revolting," she said, and shook her head in disbelief. In all her days, no matter how at odds she and her mother might have been, she could never have imagined Queen Eseld offering herself to one of Gwendolyn's intendeds.

Málik's lips curled into a bitter smile. "Such is the nature of the Fae Court. Ambition and desire blur the lines of propriety. And though it is sometimes said that all is fair in love and war, amidst this court, those things are wholly interchangeable."

"I am not worried."

He paused, his eyes meeting hers across the room. "You should be. I may keep you safe within these halls, but to keep you here eternally will make me a *gaoler* and no better than Locrinus. And if something should ever happen to me—"

"It won't," Gwendolyn said.

She padded over to the wardrobe to retrieve the dragon-scaled book, deeming this the right time to show him. "Look," she said, holding up the tome. "I have *no* fear of what the Rite of Blood will bring because I *know* the truth."

He gazed at her in surprise.

"You found it?"

She nodded.

"Read it?"

She nodded again. "I *am* of the blood," she said, smiling. "This tome holds our history—yours and mine, separate and combined."

"So you know?"

"Not quite everything," she allowed. "But given time, I will. For now, I know enough, and this book is a gift beyond measure. I will cherish it always, Málik. I will learn from it. And no matter that I do not *look* like Curcog, I will be her in more than spirit. Her memories will be mine."

He nodded. "It was a wedding gift from my grandmother," he said. "Though it will only reveal what transpired before that day."

Gwendolyn smiled compassionately. "I could never measure the worth of this sacrifice—this precious, precious gift. It is almost as though she knew I would need it someday."

"She did," he said. "My grandmother was an oracle." His expression turned faraway. "She had already had one failed escape, and her exile and imprisonment were too much to bear—but that is also why I fear keeping you imprisoned within Tech Duinn, Gwendolyn. It will diminish you eventually."

"Whatever my fate, Málik, I will be grateful for the time with you, and I have the Druids and the Púca as well. This is not the same as what Locrinus did to me."

He was silent for a moment.

"You understand that, don't you? I have come here willingly, and I will stay here willingly, and whatever my fate, I shall embrace it."

He nodded, seemingly a bit more appeased.

"Can't we show this to them? Doesn't it not prove everything?"

"No," he said. "That tome will only reveal what it wishes to reveal. And even if it did, you would betray our true names and provide them with the means to compel us. No one can know you are truly Curcog—no one but those who already know. Esme, your father..." He trailed off.

"Yes, that is true," Gwendolyn agreed, still thinking.

She knew her father had, for a good reason, introduced her to the court as Niamh of the Golden Hair, eschewing her true name, just as no one knew Málik's, or Esme's. Esme was not Esme. Her true name was Gráinne.

She carried the book back to the bed and sat for a moment, nibbling at her lower lip, trying to think of some other way to use the book.

What if there could be a witness she trusted to whom she could show the book? *Who would it be? Only Esme,* she determined. But Esme wasn't here.

She trusted the Druids, but the Fair Folk did not...and she

would give them yet another reason to dispose of them. Sighing, Gwendolyn closed the book, her fingers brushing the cover as she considered more possibilities. "If not this way, how do we convince the court?"

Málik's sigh was deep. His hands clenched and unclenched at his sides as he contemplated their limited options. "Knowing and proving are two different things," he said. "The Rite demands more than words."

"Blood?" she said.

"There is another way."

"What?"

"Manifestation."

"So if I could somehow change myself?"

"Without artifice," he said. "A glamour will only work on mortals."

Considering that, her Gwendolyn's fingers found and pushed at her canines, as though by sheer force of will, she could coerce them into forming. But of course, nothing happened.

No matter how she wished to, she couldn't change her appearance at will.

She was still, as previously determined, as mortal as Loc —the age lines forming about her eyes could attest to that. Málik was right. Words and actions were not the same.

He sauntered to the bed, his fingers finding the thorny cloak that Gwendolyn had worn, tracing the sharp points— as though he, too, were thinking the same. But how ludicrous that she considered plucking out every thorn and establishing them in her mouth. How silly a thought, but how desperate she was...

"They will not rest until Lirael has claimed what she believes is owed to her."

"Well...is *it* owed to her?"

Málik's eyes flashed. "How can you ask such a thing?"

"I only wondered if—"

"I promised her nothing," he assured. "My heart belongs to you, Gwendolyn." He came to her then, reaching for her hand, his touch gentle despite the turmoil in his eyes. "I swear to you, no words of love or commitment were ever exchanged between us. Lirael may have coveted the crown, but it was never hers to claim." Gwendolyn nodded as he knelt before her, taking both her hands in his.

Her heart skipped a beat as she stared at their fingers entwined.

The contrast between his pale, almost luminescent skin and her sun-kissed complexion was stark in the dim light of his room—still more evidence of her mortality...that the sun could burn her delicate, mortal flesh. Even her skin could die...

"I haven't any clue how to prove myself," she confessed at last.

His gaze snapped to hers, his ice-blue eyes softening. "I blame my—"

She saw regret in his eyes. "Don't," she said, and she reached out, her fingers touching his beautiful lips. "We *will* find a way," she whispered. "I did not come all this way for naught."

He swallowed, inclining toward her, his lips unerringly finding hers, and bestowing a slow, gentle kiss. Gwendolyn's lips parted with a soft moan, and their tongues danced together...until she withdrew.

"What of my father?" she pressed. "Can he speak for me?"

Málik shook his head. "Manannán mac Lir is not welcome here, though even if he could traverse the Veil, there is no one who will accept his word when it was his scheming that exiled us to this place."

Gwendolyn's hand fell away, a frown creasing her brow, the heaviness of their predicament settling over her like a heavy cloak, suffocating in its weight. She turned her face, and Málik drew her up from the bed, turning her about and wrapping his arms around her waist.

Sighing, Gwendolyn leaned back into his embrace as he nuzzled the soft skin of her neck, his warm breath sending shiver after shiver down her spine. "Do you feel that?" he asked, and his meaning was not lost to her. How could she not?—forsooth. It took her back to another time, before her uncle's house in Chysauster...before the raid on his village... when Málik held a blade to the small of her back, pressing with intent. A thrilling blend of danger and desire had coursed through her, even as now.

Even despite this situation, she felt an answering warmth between her thighs. "Yes," she whispered, her voice barely audible. She nodded, pressing herself back against his arousal.

"I have been this way since the moment I laid eyes on your beautiful face. So, it seems... not even the court's challenge may diminish my hunger for you, love..."

"Málik..."

"I would so much prefer putting this beast to use..."

Gwendolyn purred. "We can," she said. "Put it to use... worry about this later?" It was more a question than a suggestion. Gwendolyn didn't wish to confess how desperate she was to feel him atop her, inside her—to know the consummation of so many years spent apart, melded into a single moment of pure, unbridled bliss. His lips touched her ear, his whisper ragged with desire.

"We could," he whispered, his hands beginning to explore the contours of her body, tracing every line and curve, and Gwendolyn tilted her head back to grant him better access to her throat, feeling the hardness of his desire pressing more firmly against her rear.

With a gentle hand, Málik untied the laces of her gown, allowing the soft silk to slip from her shoulders, and she turned to face him, wanting to see him— wanting him to see the hunger in her own eyes. Their gazes locked as his hands continued their exploration, cupping her half-naked breasts before trailing his fingers down to the curve of her hips, pausing there for a long, delightful moment to feast his eyes on her before walking her back to the edge of the bed and lowering himself to his knees, then pulling her down and her skirts up to place shocking little kisses along the insides of both her thighs.

Gwendolyn gasped with delight.

Blood and bloody bones.

It felt so good to be in his arms...

To feel his touch again.

Her fingers tangled in his hair—soft as silk—as he

lavished more attention on her most sensitive of places, her breath coming in quick gasps of pleasure.

For all its troubles, the world beyond this chamber faded away, leaving only the exquisite sensation of Málik's lips and tongue against her flesh. He suckled, then lapped and kissed, sipping of Gwendolyn's body, and all she could do was sit with her fingers curled within his locks, her world narrowing to nothing but sensation, as her body trembled with wave after wave of pleasure. Málik's skilled ministrations brought her to the edge of bliss, and she cried out his true name as ecstasy claimed her—for the first time.

Málik caught her easily, rising with a throaty chuckle, and then tossing her back onto the bed—their bed—before laying down with her, his ice-blue eyes darkening with desire as they roamed her form.

"My beautiful, magnificent queen," he whispered with affection.

The locket about his neck swung suddenly between them, catching the light, and Gwendolyn reached for it, her fingers curling around the warm gold. She brought it close, studying the etchings carved into its surface.

He smiled, a gentle warmth in his eyes. "Open it," he said softly.

"Now?" Her voice trembled.

He nodded once. So she picked at the small lock until it yielded with a click. It fell open in her palm, revealing within a curl of golden hair.

Her breath caught. But Málik did not wait for words; his mouth lowered to the apex between her thighs, and his tongue danced along her flesh as Gwendolyn's fist closed tight around the locket, snapping it shut as he drew gasps and shudders from her lips.

He'd kept a lock of her hair. All these years, he'd kept her close, pressed to his heart. The knowledge squeezed at her, sharp and sweet. Revelation swirled within her, an epiphany blooming like dawn after endless night. Tears pricked at her eyes as Málik's touch stoked a fire within her.

"I feared I would never hold you again," he murmured between kisses, his voice roughened by longing. "Never to taste your lips...the sweet nectar of your flower..." His words, low and fervent, sent heat spiraling through her.

"My heart never left you, Málik, even when our realms divided us," she whispered, a tear slipping down her cheek. He rose at once, brushing it away with his lips before their mouths met again—a kiss soft, reverent, and trembling with all the yearning and relief Gwendolyn had carried, the ache of separation melting away like snow in spring.

He tasted familiar...

He tasted of her.

Her arms tightened around him, drawing him close as though she could merge their souls, and, as their kiss deepened, Málik's fangs grazed her lower lip, eliciting a gasp from Gwendolyn.

The prick of blood, rich and sweet, ignited a primal need within him, she knew, and he drew back uncertainly, his pale-blue eyes swirling with a preternatural light.

"Let go," she whispered, and he groaned low in answer, the sound one of pain...as though the act of restraint were tearing him apart from within. He was still wearing his leather breeches, so she understood it wasn't their physical consummation he craved so much...only one more carnal.

"Let go," she begged, reaching up, her fingers tracing the contour of his cheek.

"I will not lose you again," he said, his avowal fervent. "Not to Lirael, nor to the Shadow Court, but there are things you must understand before I take what I desire from you..."

"I already understand," she said. "I am yours," she avowed, cupping his beautiful, chiseled face in her hands, her thumbs brushing over his high cheekbones.

"And you are mine," she added as she pulled him down, their lips meeting once more. Málik's fangs scraped her lips, only this time with intent, sending shivers of anticipation down Gwendolyn's spine.

She wanted him to drink of her...

Wanted to drink of him...

She tilted her head, offering herself completely, and he scrambled backward. But just when Gwendolyn feared he would deny her and leave, he shrugged out of his leathers and stood for a moment, his eyes hazy with passion, still giving her fair warning. "We are beasts of another sort," he told her. "But animals just the same."

"I know," she whispered, eager for what was to come.

"No less primal in our need..."

Gwendolyn nodded, and with another growl, Málik returned to position himself atop her. Only rather than be afraid, Gwendolyn gazed up at him lovingly, needing him desperately.

If he was a beast, so too, was she.

Naked and unashamed, he reached between them,

brushing two fingers between her folds, then to himself, bathing himself with her silk, stroking himself as Gwendolyn watched...

He was magnificent.

Unbridled.

Unashamed.

Gwendolyn's heart beat wildly as his eyes locked with hers, full of promise.

"Well, well! So it appears...someone's been busy while I was away!" came a familiar voice, and the teasing shattered their private sanctuary like a stone through glass.

Gwendolyn shoved Málik away, cheeks flushing crimson, to face the intruder.

CHAPTER
FOURTEEN

Arrogant and unapologetic, stood Esme, her lissome frame vibrating with barely suppressed laughter. An impish grin trembled across her lips as she stood, hip cocked, with one hand on her hip.

"Oh, please, please! Do not allow me to interrupt," she pleaded, her voice honeyed and lucid with delight at their nudity. "By all means—carry on! I love a show."

Blood and bones.

Esme was a deviant.

Her coppery hair was mussed and wild as though she, too, had only just extricated herself from a lover's embrace. Neither Gwendolyn nor Málik had an immediate response for her, and Gwendolyn was so shocked she didn't think to dress. Satisfied that she had adequately made a proper entrance, Esme strutted the rest of the way into the chamber, completely without invitation, her fiery hair bouncing around her "Did you miss me?" she quipped, her green eyes alight with mischief. "Or were you too...*preoccupied* to think of me at all?" She waggled her brows.

And then, she added plaintively, "Well, so clearly, you *were* too preoccupied to send word of Gwendolyn's return. I had to hear it for myself."

Gwendolyn blinked, meeting her sister's gaze with a mixture of exasperation and fondness. "Your timing is impeccable as always, Esme."

"Indeed," agreed Málik. "One would almost think you'd planned your entrance." He levered himself up and glowered at both of them at once—mayhap because Gwendolyn couldn't quite wipe the embarrassed grin from her face. Gods knew this was not how she'd wished to meet her sister again, but she was relieved to see her. In fact, her timing couldn't be more serendipitous. She wasn't being entirely facetious. They could use her help right now.

For her part, Esme gave a very unladylike snort—a signature laugh, that one that sent most men scrambling for weapons or wine. Sometimes both.

"Is that any way to welcome your sister?" she said directly to Málik.

"*You* are *not* my sister," he argued.

"Whatever—ex-lover."

His frown deepened. "That was long ago, and my worst mistake!"

"Your worst? Really?" Esme glanced down at his stubborn erection, his desire barely diminished even with her arrival, and grinned. "I would say more delightful, as I recall —pardon Gwendolyn." She winked at Gwendolyn.

"I see your tongue is sharp as ever," Málik returned, clearly annoyed.

"Indubitably, it is part of my charm," Esme allowed, and then her grin widened. "But fear not, brother...er, lover...in-law... Majesty—I am *not* here to rekindle old flames. And I was not speaking to you. I was speaking to *her*."

Her gaze turned to Gwendolyn, softening. "I can see I've interrupted quite the reunion," she allowed with an approving smile, and her eyes slid brazenly over Gwendolyn's exposed breasts, her green eyes twinkling with mirth. "And I really must confess that shade of pink suits you."

Gathering her wits at last, Gwendolyn arose, realizing that Esme intended to remain until she had her say. She retrieved a soft-gray robe that had been laid atop the bed for her—how; she didn't know. It was as though the room itself sensed her needs. Her cheeks burning as she dressed, she fumbled with the ribbons as Málik dressed as well, less eager.

Reaching for his discarded tunic, he shot Esme a withering glance, and another smile tugged at Gwendolyn's lips. "I trust there's a reason for this...drama?"

"How did you know I was here?" Gwendolyn asked.

Smiling, Esme flounced to the bed, plopping herself down upon it, unperturbed by Málik's glare. "Manannán," she said. "He was concerned—as a father should be."

Gwendolyn couldn't deny the gratitude that washed over her at hearing this. But then again, somehow, the thought of her father—or any father—here in this room right now, whether in spirit, or in the flesh, did not suit her. Really, it should not suit her that Esme was here either, and she should be far more chagrined, but she was not. It was difficult to be embarrassed by anything in Esme's presence, when at their first meeting, Esme had so rudely squeezed her breast.

"More to the point," Málik said crossly. "Where have *you* been?"

Esme's demeanor shifted only slightly, her playful visage fading into a more serious mask. "The Lands of Eternal Winter," she revealed. "Let me tell you, Málik, it was *no* thrill. While we sit here pining for our lost homelands, it is not as I remember. There is no peace in that place—neither is the climate suitable to my liking. Cold. Bitter. The Grypes and Wyrms are endlessly at war—and I do mean endlessly!"

Málik blinked without pity, and if he was surprised by all that she'd revealed, he didn't let on. Esme continued. "The Arimaspoi appear intent upon losing their only eye, and the elves have barricaded the upper valleys. Meanwhile, Old Habetrot circles above their wards like a rook awaiting carrion."

"Who is Old Habetrot?" Gwendolyn asked.

"You don't want to know," said both Esme and Málik at once.

"And worse," Esme continued. "The Lands of Eternal Spring are infested by shrieking will-o'-the-wisps. I hopped three realms in a fortnight simply to avoid them, seeking oblivion or a decent vintage. Found only the former. Now—" she fixed both of them with a meaningful look—"I believe I'd rather be here."

"What do you mean, hopped?" Gwendolyn asked.

Esme shrugged. "Ask your lover. It is something he seems quite intent upon avoiding, choosing to do everything in the most laborious manner imaginable."

Málik's brows collided. "I have feet," he allowed.

Gwendolyn lost herself for a moment, still wondering what Esme meant by "hopped."

No doubt, there had been many times when she had suspected the Fae had other means to travel, and she even implied as much the night that Málik returned to their camp after doing Gods knew what to Loc's men. "What business took you there?" he asked, and Esme replied saucily, her voice tinged with a mix of excitement and trepidation.

"Your father's business. I tracked him, hoping to unravel the mystery of his disappearance. And let me tell you, Málik, that Wyrm knows how to cover his tracks!"

Gwendolyn blinked with surprise. "Your father lives?"

Apparently, today was a day for revelations.

"So it seems," said Málik. "But what business was that of yours, Esme? If my father wished to reveal himself, he would have done so long ago, and yet he does not. Clearly, he finds no cause to return."

Gwendolyn's gaze did not leave Málik's face, watching curiously as a tempest of emotions played across his features. *Joy, confusion, anger, hope*—each taking a turn.

So, his father lived, and Málik was not surprised, but he was angry.

"I thought you would be pleased." Esme pouted, surveying Málik through heavy lashes. "You said you would sell your soul to know if he lived," she added. "I didn't sell mine, but I spent it, Brother, and I spent more of myself than you will ever know—all for you."

For a moment, the mask dropped from Esme's face—a flicker, a wince, not precisely one of pain nor of shame but of a weariness so old that even her bottomless well of bravado ran dry. "He's been in hiding," she offered petulantly. "But that is not all."

She paused, her green eyes glinting with animosity. "Lord Elric knows where he is—he has always known. He and *his* Shadow Court made a deal with your father."

"What deal?"

Esme shrugged. "If he left, and if Aengus should somehow be dethroned... and... if you should then wed his daughter... he would lie for him and claim he was dead and gone, instead of... well, killing him." A weighty silence fell between them.

Esme turned to Gwendolyn. "That was his penance. He was to have been executed, and Lord Elric was the one to do it. But he took him into the Forbidden Lands and returned with the ceremonial dagger covered in blood—apparently no one even considered asking if he was dead, or simply wounded. After the portals were closed, I asked him about it, and he danced around the truth. So I knew."

Málik's face hardened, his ice-blue eyes turning as cold as the winter winds of his father's refuge. "So, the Shadow Court's machinations run deeper than we thought," he said, his voice low and dangerous. "And clearly, my father agreed to it."

Esme shrugged. "He fled, at least? More than that, we do

not know, and I asked why, but he would not say." Gwendolyn's heart ached for Málik.

"Did you speak to him?"

"Oh, yes," Esme said. "He was...reluctant... at first. But you know I can be persuasive when I wish to be." Her lips curved slightly.

"Will you make me ask?" Málik growled. "What did he say?" Once again, Esme's gaze flicked between Málik and Gwendolyn, her expression uncharacteristically somber. "He spoke of regret, Málik. Choices made in haste. Bargains he wished he could undo. But little more than that. He was grief-stricken over your mother, and with her death found no cause to live. But he also speaks of a threat... to you. When he heard that the two of you—" She pointed to both Gwendolyn and Málik— "Were parted, and the portals closed, he feared Lord Elric would finally have his way."

Silence.

"All I truly know is that he fears what the Shadow Court might do if he returns, and he fears that even more than he fears your wedding Lirael Silvershade."

Málik nodded, his jaw working furiously. "*She* issued a challenge."

"Lirael?"

He nodded again. "Gwendolyn—"

Esme interrupted. "Yes, I know. This is why I am here. I have a plan."

"*You* have a plan?" Gwendolyn asked.

"Really, don't look so surprised!" Esme protested.

"What plan?" Málik demanded, and Esme cast him a narrow-eyed glance.

"You must learn to trust me, Brother!"

"Once again, not your brother," Málik said, staring at her.

"For once, Málik, trust me. I vow to protect your bride with my life."

"And if I refuse?"

Esme's laughter rang with genuine delight. "But you won't," she said. "Because so much as you would like me to believe else wise, you trust me—face it. You know, all I have ever done—regardless of how it ever looked—I have done for *her*."

She turned briefly to Gwendolyn and smiled warmly, and Málik growled again, but he didn't disagree. "Now, what I really need you to do is—" She fluttered her hand, gesturing to the room at large. "Dress yourself and go. Leave us! Return to your Shadow Court. Convince them to alter the date of Gwendolyn's trial."

"Why?"

"To give us time, of course."

"They won't," he said.

"No, of course they won't. But in the meantime, you will interject a word here and there about how upset your bride is, and that she'll not eat, drink... *or leave this chamber*."

"She won't leave this chamber," Málik said firmly.

"Well... and I *am* upset," Gwendolyn allowed.

Only not quite *that* upset.

In truth, Gwendolyn was suddenly famished, because she now had the taste of hope in her mouth—like honey and nutmeg layered atop old sorrow, and it shocked her how easily those flavors mingled on her tongue.

"Again, I ask: Why?"

"I can *only* tell Gwendolyn," Esme maintained. "But don't worry, Málik, when you return, *she* will tell you *everything!*"

"And what will you two do in my absence?"

Esme batted her lashes. "Finish devising my plan, of course."

Málik frowned. "Will you enlighten me before I go?"

"No," returned Esme with a smile.

"She speaks true," declared another voice emanating from the center of the room. The Púca suddenly materialized in the center of the bed in his cat form. His fur shimmered between shades of shadow and light, adding a surreal edge to the already charged atmosphere. Málik's expression shifted from suspicion to reluctant acceptance as he regarded the creature.

"What is this? A fayre?"

"Well, it could be," said Esme lightly.

"So you agree with her?" he asked the Púca, his voice heavily laced with incredulity.

The Púca shrugged—as well as cats could shrug, and Málik turned on Esme. "Very well, but if any harm befalls her..."

"It won't," she promised. "I love her as much as you do."

His eyes softened now, a flicker of understanding passing over his features. "I know," he said a bit more gently, and Gwendolyn stepped closer to him, her hand finding his. "It won't be for long," she promised, her storm-gray eyes meeting his ice-blue gaze.

Málik peered once more at the Púca, and the creature swished its long tail with annoyance. "Go on," it said, and Málik relented, reining in his doubt, if not his disdain, realizing that if there was anything to be gleaned from Esme, it would only be done when he returned.

He took a moment to repair his tunic and then his hair.

"Please take your time," Esme demanded, her tone buoyant. "We girls have so much to speak of."

Gwendolyn pursed her lips, even as Málik snarled in response, but he gave no further protest. He shot one last warning glare at Esme, then stormed from the room, pulling the door hard behind him.

A crack of silence followed in his wake.

"Well..." said Esme, smiling. "That was simple enough."

Gwendolyn laughed softly as the Púca then sauntered over to settle its rear upon Esme's lap. "I have missed you both," she said.

The Púca said nothing, but purred, and Esme said, "I missed you, too. But not so much as our brooding prince. I heard tell he prowled these halls, howling like a dog without a bone."

She sighed. "I did not believe you would return, so I thought I would investigate the mystery of his father's whereabouts—cheer him, perhaps. It is good you have come home, because there is no joyful news to impart of his father. Indeed, if there is ever to be a homecoming for him, it will only be once Lord Elric is dead, and the Shadow Court is dismantled root and branch. And no matter, he is content enough where he is, and a God's life—even a demigod's—is long. There will be time."

"His father is a demigod?"

"Wyrms are *all* demigods," Esme allowed. "Málik is too.

And you, sister... well, it is not my place to tell you more. You must discover the rest for yourself."

Gwendolyn frowned. Too many secrets. Too many vows of silence. Too much left unsaid, and yet, she rested easy knowing that she had the tome now, and she wouldn't need anyone to reveal anything more. "So you said you had a plan? Do you mean to share it with me?"

Esme winked. "Of course." She pushed the Púca away and leapt up from the bed to embrace Gwendolyn, and Gwendolyn arched a brow.

"I am curious though... why would you not tell Málik? Do you not trust him?"

"Of course, I trust him!"

"Then why?"

Esme's lips curved into a sly smile. "Because if I dared, he would *never* have allowed you to leave with me, and there is something we really must do."

"Leave? How? They are preparing to arrest me!"

Esme's smile turned wicked. "Yes, well... Málik is *not* the only one with friends," Esme explained. "And sometimes, truly, it is not friends in high places we need. Dress yourself warmly," she directed. "It'll not be cozy where we go."

CHAPTER

FIFTEEN

N ot cozy—*this* was an understatement.

This was the Underland Gwendolyn remembered—dark and dank, with winding paths going every which way, and large, black spiders the length of her arm dangling from stalactites. The scent was less rot and more mineral, with a backdraft of wet iron and rank mushroom, so unlike the sweet gardens within the city proper.

They had exited Tech Duinn through another of those living tapestries, this one depicting a place that was hardly appealing—a red, glowing lake of fire set against a backdrop of charred stone enshrouded by clouds of ash. The moment Gwendolyn laid eyes upon it, she had been certain that once through, she would choke on the smell of sulfur and scorched earth, but there was only this long, endless corridor, walls slick with beads of moisture, and veins of iron and quartz reflecting faintly, like the eyes of waiting predators.

Esme seemed to know the way, and Gwendolyn followed

in silence, freezing in her boots when they unexpectedly encountered a Fae guard.

Undaunted, Esme moved to greet him, giving him something. He nodded, then stepped aside to allow passage, and Esme returned.

"Do you trust him?" Gwendolyn asked, worried. For this to work, they could not allow themselves to be caught.

"I do," said Esme. "He loathes Lord Elric."

"Why?"

"Because he once dared to woo that fool daughter of his, and for that, Elric lopped off the points of his ears." Gwendolyn winced, reaching out to touch her own phantom points.

"What did you give him?"

"A vial of mad honey made by giant bees in the Himālaya. It produces visions, a bit like pookies."

"Hmm," was all Gwendolyn said. Thereafter, they descended by stairwell deep into the caves below the city, and the further they descended, the colder it grew. Gwendolyn's breath coalesced before her, and her eyes strained against the dimming light. On Esme's insistence, she had opted for a coat, but now wished she were draped in heavy fur, and only belatedly remembered how badly she'd longed for her father's cloak the last time she was here.

This was yet another disappointing bit of proof of how very mortal she was. For her part, Esme seemed perfectly content in her vellum-thin garb. She moved along; her steps sure and silent, a stark contrast to Gwendolyn's cautious tread.

It would hardly suit her—or anyone—if she broke her

mortal bones. "The cold does not bother you?" she asked, her voice bouncing off the cavern walls.

Esme glanced over her shoulder with a smile sharp as the stalactites. "Nope," she said. "I spent more time in these warrens than a mole rat in its burrow."

Gwendolyn pulled her coat tighter about herself; the fabric was scarcely sufficient against the biting cold. The constant drip of water echoed persistently as they moved deeper into the labyrinthine passageways, her boots slipping occasionally on the slick stones. She kept one hand trailing along the rough wall for balance, her thoughts drifting to Arachne—the spider-woman who had both aided and perplexed her in equal measure.

Perhaps sensing her disquiet, Esme slowed the pace to allow Gwendolyn to catch up. And thereafter, they traveled together, speaking at length of Trevena and Bryn...

"He was heartbroken when you left," Gwendolyn provided.

"Not for long, I vow." Esme's tone was mordant, mayhap revealing more hurt than she was comfortable allowing. "He always had such a fascination with Taryn—or, rather, she with him."

A moment of contemplative silence passed between them.

"Or perhaps it was his life as a Shadow. Though Bryn always welcomed her attention."

"So you left out of jealousy?"

"Gods, no!" Esme cackled, the sound echoing eerily through the chilly cavern. "I left because it was not my place to stay, Gwendolyn. I was not born for that realm. My home is here—and I do mean *here*. So much as my kindred yearn for a return to the homelands, I remember why we left."

She pursed her lips, the half-light flickering across her aquiline features. "In truth, I could not bear the thought of loving a mortal, only to lose him in a few short years."

Truth. Gwendolyn sensed *that* was her true reason—and for the first time, she dared to consider if that was also the reason Málik did not stay to be with her. Here, she would defy age, even as a mortal, as did Emrys and Amergin, but there in the mortal lands, he would have stood by, watching Gwendolyn die—for wasn't that the journey for every human? From the moment they were born, they were destined to die.

For so long, Gwendolyn had believed Esme selfish and cruel to leave Bryn with no explanations, but now she considered her sister was a kinder soul than she herself could ever be.

"Was there anything you did not reveal about Málik's father I should know?"

"No," said Esme. "This is not his story, Gwendolyn. It is yours and Málik's. It is ours. Whatever the Dark One's reason for leaving, it has little to do with us, and it is not our way to pry."

Gwendolyn knew that was true. Demelza, her mother's maid, was right about this: The Fae were not forthcoming—not even when relations were close.

"You still haven't revealed your plan."

"It's very simple," said Esme. "We're going to see Arachne."

"Arachne?!"

"Indeed."

"Why?"

She turned to smile at Gwendolyn now. "To ask her for a *new* cloak."

"A new cloak? Why would I need another?" Gwendolyn's brow furrowed as she maneuvered through a narrow passageway. "Art certain you know where we are going?" She didn't remember any of these passages. But Esme's pace didn't falter, her gaze fixed ahead.

"The cloak she wove for you before *concealed* your true nature, yes? Well, this time, we intend to ask her to weave one that *reveals* you instead."

"And yes," she concluded. "I know where we are."

"Is that possible?"

Esme's eyes sparkled with mischief. "Everything is possible with Arachne's weaving."

"Will she do it? She—"

"She *had* to call the guards, Gwendolyn. If she had not, she would have sealed her own fate. It was *always* the plan to hand you over to Aengus without a fight. You cannot have imagined we would ever allow you to march into that hall wielding demands and a sword?"

Gwendolyn sighed. "But if that was 'the plan' all along, why didn't you save me the trouble and hand me over from the beginning, instead of leaving me to ferret my way through this wilderness of stone?"

"Everything happened as it should," Esme avowed, moving with feline grace from step to step, from ledge to ledge, and path to path. "At any rate, if Arachne knows what is good for her, she'll do as we ask. No good will ever come to her if Elric seizes the throne."

"Is that possible?"

"Yes. Why do you think I sought Málik's father so relentlessly? Your lover was out of his mind, without direction. Meanwhile, Elric was busy wooing the Shadow Court. I returned with Málik, but he did not realize. I was here only a few days before I realized something must be done about Elric."

"Twenty-two years is a long time to be gone," Gwendolyn allowed.

"In mortal years," Esme said. "But at any rate, it took me a long time to find him, and then a longer time to convince him to even speak to me. Elric holds some dark secret over the Banished Wyrm, and whatever it is, he did not wish for Málik to learn it."

"What do you think it could be?"

"I don't know," said Esme. "Everyone has secrets," she allowed. "His father should be the one to choose whether to share his. We're almost there," she said, as the path curved around a bend, then abruptly ended in another slick, uneven stairwell—this one, thankfully shorter. Esme took the lead, descending quickly, and Gwendolyn noted the air perfumed with the scent of something sweet—*what was that?*

"Where are we? What is that smell?"

"It is the path *to* the Old City," Esme explained. "No one ever uses it anymore. However, the way to Arachne's lair is shorter this way, and no one will consider you might know the way, much less how to navigate these corridors. And... the smell... it's from a plant only found at these depths."

They continued their descent; the light dimming as they moved deeper underground. The air grew cooler, but somehow sweeter with the scent.

"Arachne uses it as bait."

Gwendolyn thought about the pile of bones she'd spied in Arachne's lair and shuddered—not because of the chill.

She also remembered the sickeningly sweet scent of the Rot and wondered if this could be the same.

What travelers wandered so deep into the Underlands?

She thought of knockers and miners and wondered what role knockers played in the miners' disappearances. And was this where they ended?

And more specifically, in Arachne's pile of bones?

Their banter faded as the path before them grew more precarious, and Gwendolyn feared they would meander for days, when the spider's lair suddenly appeared. She knew it for the massive, silvery webs that covered the entrance, the glimmering strands catching the light and refracting it in mesmerizing patterns.

"Art ready?" Esme whispered.

"Yes," Gwendolyn said nervously.

But really, was she?

"Very well. Let us go visit our eight-legged friend."

The instant Gwendolyn and Esme crossed the threshold of her lair, Arachne skittered from the shadows, her eyes glinting not with malice, but with an unexpected warmth.

"Welcome, Daughter of Two Realms! Welcome!" she said. "Once again, I've been expecting you." Her countenance was beautiful as ever, with her long black hair and eyes heavily painted with kohl. Despite that, as lovely as she was, she was a terrifying blend of human and arachnid, with six woolly legs and two human arms protruding from human shoulders. She moved to hug Gwendolyn and, as alarming as the thought might have once been, Gwendolyn not only allowed the embrace, but returned it.

"I am sorry for betraying you to Aengus," said Arachne, as she squeezed, hard—so hard that Gwendolyn feared she would pop!

"No need," said Gwendolyn, with a heartfelt sigh. "I understand." If all things were connected, it applied no less to circumstance. She was beginning to understand every piece of this vast puzzle. Even Arachne's betrayal had been an act of kindness.

Esme cleared her throat impatiently. "As touching as this reunion may be, time is of the essence. We need your help, Arachne."

Releasing Gwendolyn, Arachne stepped back to appraise Gwendolyn with keen, dark eyes. "I know," she replied, gesturing for them to follow into her lair. "You need a new cloak."

"Can you provide it?" Gwendolyn asked.

"Of course, Child," Arachne said, in very much the same tone Demelza had so often used to address her. "However, you must use it carefully. Once you decide what you want, simply place the cloak about your shoulders. But you *must* be certain what you want, because you can lie to yourself, but you cannot lie to the cloak."

"What will it cost me?"

Arachne's answering cackle echoed through the cavern. "Cost you? Child, the question isn't what it will *cost*, but what you will gain—or lose. Art prepared for the Court to see you as you are? Can you deny your mortal lands, forsake your beloved Cornwall? The cloak will know, and make no mistake, whatever it decides, that is who you will be."

Arachne's many-jointed fingers danced through the air, gesturing wildly, and then she stopped to retrieve a length of cloth that lay upon a stool.

"Here," she said, holding up the cloak. She paused before handing it over. "But be warned... and be prepared."

"She is," Esme asserted. "Give her the cloak. Really, Arachne, must you make every presentation so dramatic?"

"Would you begrudge me?" said Arachne, and Esme shook her head. Arachne smiled.

Nervous now, Gwendolyn's blue-gray eyes met Arachne's black ones, and then her sister's green ones, searching. "How can you be so certain I am ready?"

A wry smile tugged at Esme's lips. "Because you possess something we never had—a warm, beating heart. And this is your strength, Gwendolyn, not your weakness."

Her expression softened. "Besides... you have me."

"The Shadow Court will underestimate you," predicted Arachne. "Use it to your advantage." And then, at last, she handed Gwendolyn the cloak.

Unlike Arachne's first gift, and more like the tapestries, there was nothing common to this cloak. The air hummed with magic, and the pearlescent fabric rippled like liquid starlight, casting prismatic reflections across the walls of the lair.

Gwendolyn's fingers trembled as she reached out to touch the shimmering fabric, marveling over its incredible design. It felt cool to the touch, like water made solid. "Breathtaking," she whispered, and all her fears were momentarily assuaged in the presence of such beauty.

Esme whistled. "Well, if *that* doesn't make the court take notice, I don't know what will."

Arachne released the cloak, and Gwendolyn said gratefully, "How can I ever thank you?"

"For what, Child?"

"For this gift... for your wisdom... for your friendship... it means more than words can express."

"You will thank me by facing that viper of a court with your head high, Gwendolyn. Show them the strength that lies in being one's true self... and then, later..." She grinned. "If it pleases you, perhaps you may loosen the terms of my exile. No doubt, I prefer to remain here—this place is more to my liking. Yet I do so crave the court now and again, and I may even return to weaving tapestries."

Gwendolyn nodded. "Consider it done."

"How far we have come," Arachne purred, her silken hair shining against the golden light of her cavern, as she stepped back to allow Gwendolyn to leave with the gift of her cloak. Clutching it to her breast, Gwendolyn gave a nod to Esme.

"Art ready?" asked Esme.

Gwendolyn nodded again, but as they turned to leave, she turned once more to the spider-woman. "Thank you," she said warmly.

"Art welcome," Arachne said, and thereafter, Gwendolyn and Esme took their leave, hoping to be back before Málik came looking.

"You know," said Esme after they had departed, her tone

uncharacteristically sober, "I will stand by you, no matter what happens in that cesspool of a court."

Gwendolyn felt a surge of affection for her half-sister. "I know," she said with certainty, because she did. Through everything, Esme had been there for her... the first to stand in her defense—even against Málik when the occasion demanded.

"Art nervous?"

"I am," Gwendolyn admitted. "I am only wondering... if I will still be...me."

Esme snorted, a sound that was oddly comforting in its familiarity. "Please! You will *always* be maddeningly you. But it might interest you to know how little any of it changed you as Gwendolyn. Now is your moment of truth, Gwendolyn."

CHAPTER
SIXTEEN

Upon returning to the city, Gwendolyn and Esme entered through the city gates—the same gates Gwendolyn was once paraded through by a horde of rude Fae. Only this time, there were no witnesses to her abasement.

No Fae, few *piskies*, no trolls, no brownies—only the whisper of their footsteps echoing through a peaceful lane.

Their passage went unimpeded.

It was difficult to believe she was voluntarily marching herself to the King's Hall, where so long ago they'd hung her from a gilded cage. But on this day, unlike that day, Gwendolyn would march proudly, with her head held high.

But she knew this should not be so easy.

The cloak on her arm lay as light as a breath, still heavy as a king's ransom. She could feel its power thrumming, eager to be used, but for now, she held it close, cleaving to the last vestiges of her mortal self, strangely reticent to abandon her human form, now that she understood what was to come.

Every step toward the King's Hall invited both hope and regret—for her mother, for Habren and Bryn, for Taryn, for Ely, and for a hundred thousand Cornish souls whose lives Gwendolyn had defended and shaped.

Gods knew, if Málik's love was her soul's true north, Cornwall had been her beating heart—a land rugged and wild, fierce as the sea that pounded its shores.

But she had willingly left and wanted more than anything to be with Málik—would the cloak understand?

She and Esme walked in silence, Esme's gait filled with more confidence than Gwendolyn's. Until they approached the massive doors of the King's Hall, and Esme stopped, glancing at Gwendolyn, her expression sober. "Remember, whatever happens... you are not alone." Her hand reached out to squeeze Gwendolyn's once before releasing it.

Blood and bones.

If the central plaza felt abandoned, the King's Hall was not. It was thick with creatures by the time they arrived. Word of Gwendolyn's impending trial had already spread, and the court was clearly eager to witness a spectacle.

Whispers rose in tide:

"Is that her?"

"Where is the king?"

"Why is he not with her?"

"Is that Esme?!"

"Where has she been?"

"Is the king dead?"

Dead?! Gwendolyn threw Esme a glance filled with terror,

horrified to think that they might have sent Málik into a trap. The mood of the Hall was that of a sepulcher. And despite that, she dared not falter, advancing with Esme falling a pace behind, her gaze registering a sea of hostile faces. And now, she noted the glitter of rings and signet blades... The subtle positioning of guards at strategic points along the hall's perimeter. Every noble family stood arrayed in their colors— incarnadine, obsidian, venomous green—and Gwendolyn was struck at once by a sense of peril.

Beautiful, treacherous creatures, here, beauty was a blade honed for courtly war, and every smile a wolf's grin. And Gwendolyn was the sacrificial lamb...

No one stepped forward to greet her.

No one barred her path.

Up on the dais, standing beside the Horned Throne, stood the entire Shadow Court, with Elric Silvershade and his daughter Lirael most prominent among them, their faces set in identical masks of cold anticipation.

Málik was not present, and his absence struck Gwendolyn harder than she might have expected. Where was he?

The trial was not supposed to be held until the morrow —or had they been gone so long? The Púca had once told her that time in the Underlands did not behave as it did in the mortal world.

Gwendolyn felt a stone settle in her stomach, cold and hard.

Was this a trap?

Was Esme a part of it?

Málik, as well?

Nay, it couldn't be so.

Gwendolyn couldn't bear that thought, but even as the Fae realm shifted time's flow, the mood of its denizens shifted more capriciously.

How many times had she wondered about Málik and Esme's loyalty...

But how many times had they proven their love?

As the weight of unease tightened around Gwendolyn, Esme leaned close and said, with a smile that was far too... *amused*? "They are ready to eat you alive, sister."

"Well, I hope it chokes them," Gwendolyn returned, never taking her eyes from the dais.

"They've wasted no time," said Esme. "Elric, the bastard."

A bell tolled somewhere, its note so low it vibrated to the marrow of Gwendolyn's bones. She continued forward with measured, deliberate steps, her pulse thrumming in her ears like a war drum, and catching sight of her, a steward rushed forward, with livery black as night—the Shadow Court?

He lifted his voice to address the hall: "Presenting herself for trial... Gwendolyn of Cornwall, Queen of Men, Consort to our King, His Majesty, Málik Danann!"

A susurration swept the assembled; no one bowed. Instead, the crowd squealed, and pressed closer. Meanwhile, on the dais, Lirael's lips parted into a sneer.

"How charming. She arrives dressed as a peasant expecting to rule."

Gwendolyn glowered at her. She'd been given no time to return to her bower to trade her travel attire for an appropriate gown. Esme insisted she wear something warm but serviceable—olive wool and undyed linen, scarcely fit for a queen. Against the glitter of gems and silks adorning the gathered nobility, Gwendolyn's costume made her look more a shepherdess than a queen. But she didn't need gems or gold.

Undaunted, she straightened her spine, lifting her chin, and silence descended, every creature's attention fixed upon her as she moved purposefully toward the dais.

Lord Elric turned. "Welcome!" he said. "I'm so pleased to see you are not so indisposed as our king would suggest. Such courage you have, to come unescorted to our court of justice. But I hope you brought something more than a mortal's pride to vindicate yourself."

Gwendolyn wanted more than anything to do what she did last time—draw her blade, slice that fool's head from his shoulders, but she'd come unarmed.

Esme did not, however. Her sister drew a blade, then pointed it directly at Lord Elric, a promise in her emerald gaze. "Choose your words well, High Lord Minister," she said. "Lest your tongue need trimming!"

Elric regarded the challenge with lazy amusement, inclining his head slightly, then flicking his gaze to the council. "The prodigal daughter returns," he said. "She who would abandon the court in its hour of need to champion a mortal queen."

"Our laws are not prone to sentiment," declared a member of the Shadow Court, a pallid senior whose robes shimmered like a trout in moonlit water.

Lord Maelon concurred and said, "Hear, hear!"

But then, he surprised Gwendolyn by adding, "It is the burden of the accused to demonstrate her claim before the eyes of all. However, Lord Elric, we shall mind our words until that time—" He shot Esme a warning glare. "As well as our blades."

"Oh, please! Let the trial commence!" Lirael exclaimed, her beauty hardened and cruel. She raised a white-gloved hand, and a hush rippled outward from the dais, stilling every motion.

"Already, she behaves as though she is queen—even without the crown," said Esme angrily. But Gwendolyn said nothing, well aware of all eyes upon her.

She steadied her breath, ignoring the derisive laughter bubbling up from the pit of the court, and clutching the Cloak of Visibility close to her breast, she advanced through the ranks, intending to take her place on the King's Dais. By the eyes of Lugh! She would not don this cloak in the thick of it all, lest her change not be witnessed and her testimony be forsworn. More than anything, she wished to be standing next to Málik when she revealed her true self, but whether he was there in body, he was here in spirit. Her steps were measured, her very demeanor a challenge to the court's scorn.

She heard Esme whisper behind her, "Stay sharp, sister." And her courage nearly faltered.

"Easy for you to say," Gwendolyn returned. "You're the one holding a blade."

"Yes, well, if I had given you one," Esme returned. "You'd be dead by now. So thank me for that later."

A single attendant appeared at the foot of the dais—this one dressed in Málik's deep-green livery, and Gwendolyn recognized him as one of the guards who had led her to the feast. He escorted Gwendolyn the rest of the way up the steps, the hush of the hall so complete that even her heartbeat seemed a trespass, and all the while, her gaze sought Málik. *Where could he be?*

At the apex, Lirael's pale blue eyes scoured her, not so much a muscle twitching to betray the delight she took in Gwendolyn's predicament.

"Well now," said Lord Elric. "Now that we are all here...."

Not everyone! Gwendolyn longed to shout, but if she raised her voice, she might weep.

"Let us proceed," Elric Silvershade announced, his voice a smooth treacle of authority that hid the venom beneath.

The entire hall echoed his sentiment with murmurs of assent.

Gwendolyn's gaze swept over the faces, finding no friend save Esme. No matter, she steadied herself, then spoke, her voice loud enough for all to hear. "I've come at your behest, Lord Ministers. You asked for proof of my birthright? So here! Witness my proof!"

Lirael, her eyes wild and sharp as splinters, barked a laugh. "How will you manage, Queenling? Will you sprout wings? Tear your flesh to show us the creature beneath?" Her laugh was a cackle, and Esme growled, ready to intervene. Gwendolyn lifted a staying hand as Esme scoffed her complaint to the Shadow Court. "They always think we are something we are not," she said. "Mortals!"

The time was now, with or without Málik.

Gwendolyn understood that, so much as he loved her, Málik could not save her. She took the cloak from her arm and shook it out, its shimmer drawing a gasp from even the most jaded. She raised it high, the way she'd once lifted the Sword of Light, and let it unfurl in the strange, cold light. And then, without ceremony, she swung it over her shoulders, playing this gambit with full awareness of the stakes.

I am home, she thought. *I want to be here. I am Curcog, but no less Gwendolyn, and I need not be anything but who I choose.*

As the fabric poured over her like water, settling along Gwendolyn's shoulders, the atmosphere of the room changed—tension though something else, as well.

On her body, the cloak had no color, instead reflecting every living hue. She pulled the cowl over her head, and the transformation began immediately.

She felt the cloak's magic crawl over her flesh, rewriting her bones, and for a long frightening moment she hovered on the threshold between worlds—a child of Cornwall... the scion of the Fae... slayer of kings... and maker of peace.

Gwendolyn closed her eyes, accepting the consequences.

Cornwall would be lost to her.

Her son as well.

But she knew with every fiber of her being that this was where she belonged.

Her body altered subtly, but noticeably.

Her skin adopted a sheen like Cornish pearls.

Her ears lengthened to elegant points.

Her features sharpened, transforming.

And when she opened her eyes again, she saw the King's Hall as though for the first time—colors sharper and the souls of her enemies and allies, all burning like cinders in a night field.

Gasps rippled through the court as the cloak revealed her true form.

Her hair, always golden, now shone like a mane of pure sunlight. Her eyes, once a stormy gray, flashed with quicksilver. The bones beneath her flesh hinted at a wilder ancestry—cheekbones cut from stone, lips that could speak either blessing or curse. But it was the aura surrounding her that staggered the assembly—the aura of a god.

And yes, it was true. She was Manannán mac Lir's daughter—but also the daughter of Ethniu, who was daughter to Balor and the mother of Lugh.

The blood of the Ancients ran through her veins.

A tremble rolled through the halls, followed by Lord Elric's suddenly pallid complexion, his eyes wide, as though seeing a shade.

Beside him, Lirael's sneer faltered. She recoiled, her mask of arrogance slipping to reveal naked fear. "This is a trick!" she spat. "An illusion—no more! She cannot be Niamh of the Golden Hair! No! No! No!"

But she was!

Oh, she was!

And now Gwendolyn could prove it.

That was the sobriquet her father gave her when she came to be Aengus' ward. No one knew her as Curcog, but Málik. She spread her arms; the cloak somehow billowing in the still air. "No trick, Lirael. This is who I am, and who I choose to be." She turned her gaze to the members of the Shadow Court, and again to the curtains behind the dais—seeking Málik. She could feel their bond simmering through her veins as the court's mutters grew into a cacophony of disbelief and awe, getting stronger and stronger by the moment as he approached.

Lirael's challenge, so venomously poised, now faltered against the inevitable truth. No longer could anyone deny her Fae ancestry, but she needed them to understand something more... because she suddenly knew what Esme had meant about her warm, beating heart. Her warm, beating *mortal* heart.

Arachne was mistaken. She was not merely a Daughter of Two Realms, as the spider woman had implied. She was the Daughter of Three!

All her memories came flooding back—*everything.*

"I will not forsake my birth, nor any right. I am Fae by blood, but human as well."

The goddess part was theirs to behold by the golden glow that emanated from her flesh, so bright it illuminated the entire room and all who stood in her presence.

She peered at Esme to see that her sister was smiling— her half-sister, who had so oft risked her life, and who gave up her own claim to the Fae throne to keep Gwendolyn safe. Turning now, she faced the court again.

"I come to you with open arms and a heart that knows the love of many realms. If you will, let this be the dawn of a new age. There are too many who would see our worlds remain ever divided—who believe strength lies in purity and tradition. But I say unto you, with surety, that strength is in love, in hope, and the future we make!"

Her words hung in the air, surprising even herself, gathering energy, swelling to every corner of the hall. One by one,

Gwendolyn spied the reactions play across the room—for some, fear and for others, hope.

The old lords of the Shadow Court conferred in harsh whispers, their calculations already shifting. Elric Silvershade smiled, a serpent's grin, and then clapped.

"Beautifully spoken, lady. But words are not enough. Where is your king? Has he abandoned you already? Or have you disposed of him to usurp his place?"

Another hush fell, then a commotion from the crowd, but Gwendolyn said nothing, feeling Málik's presence so strong that she knew he would appear any moment. Lord Elric was only desperate and too stupid to realize he had already lost.

At last, Gwendolyn peered up to see the curtain part, and there he stood! Málik, his hair wild, his eyes burning with desperation, but his gaze filled with relief at the sight of her and he halted abruptly to gaze at her... as she was.

Almost bashfully, Gwendolyn lifted a hand to the peak of her ear to find the point, and she smiled... with a mouth full of porbeagle teeth.

The silence that followed seemed to last an eternity.

Gwendolyn feared she would come undone—she had never felt so exposed, so vulnerable. As powerful as she had felt only a moment before, she was nothing if he did not love her in this new form. His eyes traversed the contours of her transformed face, his expression unreadable. The tension within the hall remained palpable, the air thick with anticipation and unspoken questions. His arrival was both a salvation and a trial in itself. And then, suddenly, he moved, his strides measured but urgent.

"My love!" he exclaimed.

"Málik!" Gwendolyn sobbed, and in that interminable moment before he reached her, before he touched her, the air between them thrummed with the intensity of their bond. Ever so gingerly, he cupped her face in two hands, his touch worshipful. And then he kissed her, deeply and fiercely, as though to proclaim his allegiance before the eyes of all. Their lips parted with the sweet taste of tears mixed with joy, and for a heartbeat, all worlds twinned in that hall.

Gwendolyn felt herself suffused with a joy so fierce it scarcely distinguished itself from pain.

No one moved to intervene.

All eyes remained upon them, and for that one tiny moment, they were two souls, flawed and whole, united before gods and creatures alike. But as no true Faerie's tale will ever unfold without treachery, Gwendolyn's moment of glory was shattered by an ear-piercing squeal.

The first to move was Lirael, her face twisting with ugly rage. She snatched up a ceremonial dagger from the dais—the one meant to cut Gwendolyn's flesh to test her blood—and flung it, point-first, at Gwendolyn's breast.

Time slowed.

Gwendolyn saw every detail in motion—the flick of Lirael's wrist, the whorls of the blade.

Esme was faster. Her sister moved like the wind, intercepting Lirael's blade with the flat of her palm. Blood sprayed, and a collective gasp rose. But Esme stood grinning through the pain, holding the ceremonial knife aloft, still embedded in her palm.

"Pathetic throw," she jeered. "Next time, why don't you

try aiming for my heart? It's harder to miss than yours, heartless bitch!"

She then turned to Gwendolyn and whispered. "This one is going to hurt, damn it. It's difficult to heal a wound from this blade."

Horrified, Gwendolyn stood watching as Lirael wailed and her father stared at the floor, refusing to meet anyone's gaze.

Old Lord Maelon said: "The Rite is done. We are satisfied. The court will abide." And then he followed his declaration with, "Guards! Arrest Lirael Silvershade!"

At once, two black-liveried guards converged upon the dais, seizing Lirael by her arms—the very support she had intended to use against Gwendolyn turning against her. She fought them, her heels clattering wildly across the floor as she struggled.

"Fools!" she shrieked. "Fools! Bloody fools! Can't you see it's a trick? She's not Fae! She's not Niamh!" She struggled desperately, her refined façade crumbling into a spectacle of misery as they dragged her away.

The hall, once divided by intrigue, now united in a murmur of approval as her father staggered backward, his obsidian eyes wide and flat with shock.

"Arrest Lord Elric as well," demanded Maelon, and several of the king's guards moved to obey, flanking the Shadow Court's guards as they dragged both the High Lord Minister and his daughter from the dais.

Lirael was still screaming when they reached the lower steps, her voice gone raw, but in the hush that followed her departure, the mood of the hall lifted.

Málik gave Gwendolyn a nod, gesturing for her to speak, and Gwendolyn turned to face the assembly, her presence now as majestic as it was serene, the cloak's magic still shimmering around her. But rather than cling to the cloak, she dared to shed Arachne's gift.

Nothing changed. She was no longer Gwendolyn, but still Gwendolyn.

"We are not the past," she declared. "We are what follows. I will stand for you, if you stand for me?" A ripple of silence traveled down the gallery, as though the assembled courtiers needed the space of three shared breaths to comprehend what had just occurred. And then, the old lords and ladies all clapped, and Málik took her by the hand.

With blood still dripping from her palm, Esme offered a cheeky salute. "Vivat Regina," she proclaimed in the language of the Gods.

In perfect echo, a thousand voices replied: "Vivat Regina!"

Their voices rebounded off the halls, until the bones of the palace itself seemed to shiver, and for a moment, even Gwendolyn was swept away by the lauds. Not since she'd won the battle against Locrinus AP Brwt had she received such a thunderous praise.

"You see?" Esme purred, sidling up beside Gwendolyn. "They are only harmless sheep, only ever needing a dragon to lead them."

She clutched her wounded hand to her breast, where it freely bled, and Gwendolyn leaned close to whisper. "I think the saying goes, 'they need a wolf.'"

Esme grinned, all fang, lunacy and pride. "Wolf, dragon,

sheep—it matters not. Today, sister, you are all three." She added in a whisper only Gwendolyn could hear, "Maybe now you may return to the business I interrupted. I promise not to intrude again."

Laughter—actual laughter, bright and buoyant—bubbled up from Gwendolyn's belly before she could suppress it, and Málik's answering smile was full of mischief.

"I will second that," he said, and with that, he caught Gwendolyn by the waist—and with a flagrant lack of royal dignity, spun her around, sweeping her off her feet as though she weighed but a feather. And in the heart of the King's Hall, with all the court as witnesses, he then pressed a victorious kiss to her mouth, after which, with the queen in his arms, he departed.

CHAPTER
SEVENTEEN

Before returning to our bower, I take Gwendolyn to what has become my favorite haunt—the bathhouse, modeled after the one in Trevena.

"So it seems...you spoke true," she says, her smile sly, her memory keen. She is thinking, I know, of the night we reclaimed Trevena from Locrinus and his brothers, and of the boast I made in the water screw.

I say nothing, only grin.

The water here, warm, infused with lavender and cedar, courses through a series of pools at different levels, each spilling into the next, the sound a soothing river song that fills the air with peace. Steam coils up, clinging to the stone walls, beading on our skin, turning the world soft and dreamlike.

Like our bower, this chamber is not a fantastical creation of Arachne's, but a sacred place, a temple to love and beauty, crafted with such precision and artistry that it felt like a living, breathing entity. The rippling pools, illuminated by soft torchlight, cast shadows against the walls and creating a mesmerizing display.

As is proper, I undress, then bathe her, restraining my ardor with a king's discipline, serving my queen with the reverence she deserves—even as the urge to seize her, and press her body to mine, pulls at my cock. The ache builds, exquisite and maddening, but I savor it, relishing the feel of her skin beneath my hands as I trace the elegant lines of her shoulders and back with the soapy cloth.

We have waited twenty-two years.

What is a handful of moments more?

The thought of taking her is a devil at my ear, whispering, tempting, but I hold fast. The gravity of this reunion demands more than haste—it demands ceremony, and the honoring of a bond once sundered by fate and time. The water enfolds us; the lavender sinking deep, unwinding the knots of our separation layer by layer. Her skin, nearly pearlescent in the mist, gleams beneath the gentle light, and I make a ritual of bathing her, a rite of renewal, as though by cleansing her flesh I may also wash away the years lost. This act, despite its intimacy, is far less about carnal desire and more a ritual of renewal, symbolizing her rebirth into our world.

Her sighs blend with the burble of the watercourse, and when she leans back against me, head pillowed on my shoulder, eyes closed, I feel the world narrow to the heat and scent and sound of her, my heart thumping wildly.

The steam dances around us, cloaking us in a private

world that hums with the promise of all the moments we've yet to share

"I've dreamt of this so long," she murmurs, her voice barely audible above the lapping water.

"As have I," I answer, my words nearly lost in the hush.

Every sweep of the cloth is an attempt to erase the scars of our past, to offer her back to herself, whole and restored.

When the bathing is done, I dry her with care—every inch of her, slowly and deliberately—then wrap her in a new robe, soft as down, and guide her through the corridors at a pace that belies the beast stirring beneath my robe.

Denied too long. There has never been another for me, but her.

At the door to our chambers, the heavy oak swings open with the barest push, and torchlight spills across the threshold, warm and golden. I have forbidden the Faerie Flames from entering this chamber tonight. No Esme, no Púca— only us, as it should be.

Within, every detail proclaims that this should be her sanctuary, prepared with a meticulousness bordering on obsession.

The door closes behind us with a gentle click, sealing us in, and for a long moment, neither of us speaks, the silence becoming a living thing, charged with all that has gone unsaid so long.

Her eyes—blue-gray, and sharp as a blade—are almost too much to bear. Every time I look into them, I am reminded how easily the fate of my kingdom, and the fate of my soul, pivots on the edge of her regard.

"Now, where were we?" I ask, my voice roughened by want.

Her chin lifts—a challenge, shattering any illusion of weakness. She has always been proud, stubborn, indomitable. This is what I love most: not her beauty, nor her power, but her refusal to break, save for the sake of others. "What should I call you now?" I ask, marveling at the transformation wrought in her.

She is Curcog, but not Curcog—her eyes, her smile, but also something new, something born of pain and time and change.

She breathes softly, not meeting my gaze at first, nervous perhaps, but not meek. "What did you call me then?"

"Lover," I growl, my need for her as plain as my fangs, which ache for her essence.

With a wolf's hunger, I press her to the wall, one hand at her hip, the other at her jaw, forcing her to meet my gaze. Her eyes—stormy, desperate—lock with mine, so raw I fear the world might shatter under the weight of it.

Gods. I can never tell if it is the mortal in her—the suffering, the endurance, the years spent holding the world together with nothing but grit—or the immortal, my immortal, whose need burns white-hot in these stolen moments.

All the memories between us congeal: the aching absences, the fleeting touches, the agony of never enough.

For too long I have waited.

Too long.

Still, I hold myself in check as her hand splays between us, breathless.

The lump in my throat is a stone.

How many nights have I lain awake, longing for this moment? How many times have I conjured her voice, her touch, only to wake to cold, empty sheets and the shameful solace of my fist? Bringing myself to a completion that never satisfied—never truly, not without her.

My hands ache to touch her, to test her wetness and prove she is real. I grin. "So here we are at last."

She nods, her smile lovely and a touch defiant. "Against all odds."

"Indeed," I whisper, pride swelling in my chest.

This is the creature I would die for, a thousand times over.

"I am glad I did not know what Esme planned," I confess. "I wouldn't have let you leave."

A beat of silence.

She shrugs. "I am glad I went."

"No regrets?"

Gwendolyn shakes her golden head, and the sight of it— her hair, her certainty—stirs my cock to pain. For so long, even the thought of her lips on mine, her body beneath me, was enough to torment me beyond reason.

"No regrets," she whispers, the words a promise, a dare. Her hand slips lower, finds my shaft, and the hunger in her palm is equal to my own.

"Whatever comes," she says, "we will face it together."

I nod. "Together," I echo, and drink her in, in no hurry to claim what I know she will give. Why rush when I never want this to end?

She takes my hand, leads me to the bed, her gaze never leaving mine.

The light—strange and spectral—limns her hair in a halo.

She is as changed as she is unchanged, and it delights me beyond all reason. I came to know and love the mortal as much as I did her counterpart.

Her hair falls into her face, and I brush it back, exposing the stubborn set of her jaw and the tremor at the edge of her lips. I want to devour that tremor, taste it, but I linger, worshipping the shape of her shoulders, the hollow of her throat, memorizing every curve anew.

She lies back, watching me, a smile turning her lips. She knows the effect she has, her eyes alive with triumph and mischief and hunger. She moves with the surety of a woman who has commanded armies, but she yields to me now, inviting me to worship at her altar.

And I do.

With infinite care, I stretch beside her, tracing the hollow above her collarbone. She shudders, exhaling a ragged breath, and my body grows harder, straining for her—no, for us. For this is not merely a union, but a reunion: her body, mine, and mine, hers.

"I've missed this... and you... so much."

It's impossible to say which of us has spoken, so complete is our accord.

Her hand covers mine, pressing it to her cheek, and the gesture is more eloquent than any vow. My heart hammers, overwhelmed by the force of what I feel. "We're here now," she says. "Together. And nothing will part us again."

The fire in her voice ignites something feral within me. With a growl, I roll atop her, pressing her body beneath mine. She melts into me, arms tight around my neck, clinging with desperation to match my own. I bury my face in the crook of her neck, inhaling deeply—her scent, lavender and spices, is a balm.

My fingers tangle in her hair, anchoring me to this moment, this reality where she is finally, truly mine again.

"My love," I whisper against her lips, feeling her shiver.

Her fingers dig into my shoulders. "My king," she breathes. "My home."

And for a time, we simply lie together, lost in the sanctuary of our embrace, my mind racing with memories—our first meeting in Aengus' court, stolen moments in moonlit gardens, the agony of our first parting. Every trial, every heartache, has led us here. Slowly, I pull back to search her eyes. "I swear to you, Gwendolyn—no force in this world or any other will part us again. And...there is a ritual," I add, voice low. "It binds two souls, intertwining our essences beyond any carnal act." My thumb traces her cheek as I speak, each circle sending a tremor through her.

"Tell me more..." Her gaze never wavers.

"Through this, we share not only our lives, but our very beings. Our strengths, our weaknesses, our magic—we are one."

She laughs, bright and wicked. "Even our bodies?"

I laugh too, the sound raw. "No. Thank the gods."

The laughter fades, and the silence that follows is thick with anticipation. I take her face in my hands, thumb caressing her cheekbone, and she leans into my touch.

"Yes," she whispers, squeezing my hand. "A thousand times, yes..."

Her words strike me like a spell. She trembles, but her gaze is iron, as though two eternities might merge in a single breath. "You understand that once done, it may never be undone? We are bound for eternity, through this life and the next?" I draw her close, eager to begin. "My brave, beautiful queen," I whisper. "You never cease to amaze me." I brush her lips with mine—a feather-light kiss, reverent with the knowledge of all we have been, and all we have lost.

My hands tremble as I map the contours of her face—the sweep of her cheekbones.

She meets my gaze. "Yes," she says again, barely more than a breath.

"Do you remember the night in the Druid village when we..."

"Yes," she says, smiling, and it is all I need.

"We started, but never finished," I say. And then slowly, I untie her robe, baring the curves of her breasts. Her nipples harden in the cool air, and my fingers trace the line of her neck. "Ready?" I ask, voice thick with hunger.

Gwendolyn nods, her heart thundering in time with mine. I lean in, lips at her ear, fangs teasing her lobe. "It may hurt, *mo chroí*," I warn, savoring the endearment.

Her pulse stutters, and she nods, eyes locked with mine —a trust so deep it shames me. My fangs graze her flesh, and she closes her eyes, bracing. I bite, sinking my teeth into the space above her heart. The taste of her—sweet, wild, absolute—floods my senses. This is communion beyond blood; it is the mingling of our very selves. I feel the moment pain surrenders to pleasure, as the Aether of my life pours into her.

My cock hardens to agony, if it were not already so. I know what she feels. I crave it for myself—that wild surge, ancient and pure, burning through her.

She gasps, her nails biting into my shoulders. "I feel... you," she breathes, awash in sensation.

I withdraw. "Your turn," I say, drawing her mouth to my chest. Her hands shake as she pulls me close, hesitating only a moment before her newly won fangs pierce the flesh above my heart. For a beat, she drinks, and it is a different pleasure —one that unmans me, her need pulling at my very soul, swallowing my essence as a star swallows light.

We gasp together, the hunger ancient and immediate, joy and grief entwined for all we have lost. She does not merely drink; she marks me, her mouth a brand, and for an instant I regret nothing—not the centuries of loneliness, not the pain. The taste of my blood is thick with memory, and the boundaries between us blur.

But that is not enough.

"Don't suck," I rasp, and when she tries to pull away, I draw her back. She understands somehow, and reverses the flow, sending her own essence—her battered, indomitable soul—into me.

My body convulses, rocked by sensation—her spirit, molten and bright, pouring through my veins. Lightning arcs through me, lava seeping through my bones, and in a flash, I see every moment we have ever shared. My breath shudders; desire—white, liquid, devouring—burns through me.

Now, filled with a need sharper than hunger, I meet her

gaze. Her storm-gray eyes, luminous and wild, reflect a love so raw it nearly undoes me.

Majesty, I think, and it is hers, not mine.

It sends a pulse of want through me, and I wrench her mouth from my skin to stare into her Aether-drunk eyes.

She nips her lower lip, and the echo of her teeth in my chest stokes my hunger. I want her—her body, her scent, her scars, and her sorrow, every secret place within her.

She falls back, dizzy, her hair spilling gold across our bed —our bed, at last. The thought fills me with savage joy.

I reach for her. All the years of longing and loss focus on the trembling of my hand. With care, I gather her hair, twist it about my fist, and draw her to me. Her breath is hot and ragged. My blood is on her lips, and beneath it, the taste of her. Our mouths meet, greedy and desperate, as though the world might end if we do not consume each other now.

My fangs prick her lip—accident or intent, I do not know —and she gasps, shuddering as a bead of crimson wells at the corner of her mouth. She laps it away, eyes locked to mine, and the sight nearly undoes me.

We lose ourselves then, tumbling into the bedclothes, tearing away the last barriers, a tangle of flesh and need. Her hands in my hair, my palms at her back, her thighs caging my hips. Nothing in this world, or any other, could keep me from her now. I claim her mouth, addicted to the taste, the salt of her skin. Her hands are never idle, scoring my back.

Another heartbeat, and we are joined—slick, hot, perfect —her hips rising to meet me, our breaths tangled. The first thrust is a homecoming, bodies aligned as they were always meant to be.

She moans my name—my true name—and clings to me, nails raking my spine. Every muscle strains, desperate to prolong the moment, but helpless before the hunger that drives us. She holds me so fiercely I fear she will break me, but I crave it.

Her scent is dizzying, more potent than wine.

When I lower my lips to her throat, she bares it, sighing my name as though it is the only word left in her. My teeth graze her pulse, and she trembles. But I do not bite—not yet. I want the tension to build, to drive us both to the edge. By the time I taste her, the world has shrunk to this bed, this room, this moment. The stone walls vanish; only the heat between us remains.

I bite gently, drawing her blood, and the taste is ecstasy—memory, emotion, power, all at once.

Gwendolyn moans, low and shuddering, pain and pleasure inseparable, her nails locking me to her.

And in that instant, I find my completion with a howl that rips from my chest, wild and unrestrained. She matches me, pulse for pulse, until we are both spent, shattered, and remade.

Together, we collapse, tangled in sweat and linen and joy. Only our softly panting breaths break the silence, slowing, settling into the easy cadence of lovers at peace.

Her heart beats in my ear as I rest against her, and if I could remain here for a thousand years, I would. The sense of wholeness is overwhelming. For too long, I have borne the weight of my blood—son of the Dark One, heir to shadows—but now, with her light woven through mine, the burden is lighter.

"What are you thinking?" Gwendolyn asks, sensing the shift.

I draw a long, shuddering breath. "I... am thinking of all we have endured to reach this moment. The Shadow Court, the divide between our worlds..." I trail off, brow furrowing. "And yet, here we are, united. At last..."

"A victory for us," Gwendolyn finishes, her voice fierce. "One of many to come, my love."

I turn to her, finding my resolve mirrored in her stormy eyes. I cup her face, thumb stroking her cheekbone.

"A victory indeed, *mo ghrá*," I whisper, voice thick. She leans into my hand, golden hair spilling over my fingers, and a swell of emotion threatens to drown me—love, pride, determination. "You have always been my light," I confess. "Even in darkness, your spirit has carried me. Now, with our essences joined, I am invincible."

She smiles, mischief in her eyes. "Invincible... but not inexhaustible," she purrs, and then she is upon me, pinning me beneath her, smile predatory.

Her knees trap my arms, thighs strong as iron. Her hair falls about us, a golden veil, and I say, "I wouldn't have it any other way."

I am transfixed by the sight of her above me—warrior, queen, goddess incarnate. I reach up, and she lets me tangle my fingers in her hair, lets me draw her down for another kiss. Desire surges, white-hot, obliterating all but her, this, and the eternity of our bond.

The taste of her is new again, and I am consumed by the animal joy of surrender, of belonging wholly to her.

My love for her is beyond measure.

"Once more," she whispers, and then bends, her teeth at my throat, and I swear she means to devour me. I cry out, not in pain, but in the savage joy of being unmade and remade by her hands. And when at last we collapse, entwined in the afterglow, peace settles over us. The world outside fades to nothing as I close my eyes, and together we drift into a shared dream, ready to face whatever tomorrow brings— certain that, together, we are unstoppable.

A Heartfelt Thank You!

If you've gotten this far, then thank you from the bottom of my heart for reading The Goldenchild Prophecy. If you enjoyed this book, please consider posting a review. Reviews don't just help the author, they help other readers discover our books and, no matter how long or short, I sincerely appreciate every review.

Would you like to know when my next book is available?
Sign up for my newsletter:

♥ Thank you! ♥

TANYACROSBY.COM/SUBSCRIBE

Also, please follow me on BookBub to be notified of deals and new releases.

Let's hang out! I have a Facebook group:

Thank you again for reading and for your support.

Tanya Anne Crosby

ALSO BY TANYA ANNE CROSBY

THE GOLDENCHILD PROPHECY

The Cornish Princess

The Queen's Huntsman

The Forgotten Prince

Arise the Queen

A Crown So Cursed

DAUGHTERS OF AVALON

The King's Favorite

The Holly & the Ivy

A Winter's Rose

Fire Song

Lord of Shadows

THE PRINCE & THE IMPOSTOR

Seduced by a Prince

A Crown for a Lady

The Art of Kissing Beneath the Mistletoe

THE HIGHLAND BRIDES

The MacKinnon's Bride

Lyon's Gift

On Bended Knee

Lion Heart

Highland Song

MacKinnon's Hope

GUARDIANS OF THE STONE

Once Upon a Highland Legend

Highland Fire

Highland Steel

Highland Storm

Maiden of the Mist

THE MEDIEVAL HEROES

Once Upon a Kiss

Angel of Fire

Viking's Prize

REDEEMABLE ROGUES

Happily Ever After

Perfect In My Sight

McKenzie's Bride

Kissed by a Rogue

Thirty Ways to Leave a Duke

A Perfectly Scandalous Proposal

One Knight's Stand

ANTHOLOGIES & NOVELLAS

Lady's Man

Married at Midnight

The Winter Stone

Romantic Suspense

Leave No Trace

Speak No Evil

Tell No Lies

Mainstream Fiction

The Girl Who Stayed

The Things We Leave Behind

Redemption Song

Reprisal

Everyday Lies

ABOUT THE AUTHOR

Tanya Anne Crosby is the New York Times and USA Today bestselling author of more than forty novels. She has been featured in magazines, such as *People, Romantic Times* and *Publisher's Weekly*, and her books have been translated into eight languages. Her first novel was published in 1992 by Avon Books, where Tanya was hailed as "one of Avon's fastest rising stars." Her fourth book was chosen to launch the company's Avon Romantic Treasure imprint.

Known for stories charged with emotion and humor and filled with flawed characters Tanya is an award-winning author, journalist, and editor, and her novels have garnered reader praise and glowing critical reviews. She and her writer husband split their time between Charleston, SC, where she was raised, and northern Michigan, where the couple make their home.

For more information

Website
Email
Newsletter